TICH
Vampire Hunter

Also by Pete Barrett

Tich Dragonslayer

TICH
Vampire Hunter

Pete Barrett

Published by playbackbooks
213 St John's Road, Colchester CO4 0JG

First published 2012

1 3 5 7 9 10 8 6 4 2

Text copyright © Pete Barrett, 2012

The moral right of the author has been asserted

A CIP catalogue record for this book is available
from the British Library

ISBN 978-0-9570502-1-1

Printed in Poland

www.petebarrett.co.uk

Chapter One

Grave Expectations

There was general agreement between Tich, Ginger, Maggs and the Boff that life had been a bit boring lately. A few years ago this wouldn't have been the case but, since the *Imaginator* had come along and they'd had adventures with a baby dragon and fought soldiers alongside Robin Hood, the whole thing about hanging about the Mall, throwing stones at the Tesco trolley in the canal and playing hide-and-seek among the old disused warehouses – 'Entrance Strictly Forbidden' – just seemed to have become a bit monotonous.

School of course was, had always been and would always be, monotonous, but that was as it should be. You didn't go to school to have fun, you went to school so that the rest of life could seem, in contrast, to be absolutely brilliant.

But now everything seemed as grey and drizzly as the weather. Even dodging the Goons no longer had their hearts beating. Pigboy, Barf and Thicko had all been suspended from school and they were keeping a low profile, only managing a little light bullying and the occasional taunt to keep themselves in practice, until such time that they returned to school and were able to resume their reign of terror.

On Saturday morning, having spent all their money in the Mall, Tich and the gang began the long walk home. As they passed St Swithin's Church, Ginger said, 'Ooh look it's a graveyard. I bet there's monsters in there.'

His three friends stopped and stared at him. 'Why would there be monsters in a graveyard?' asked the Boff.

''Cause it's spooky,' replied Ginger.

'It's ghosts you get in a graveyard,' explained the Boff, 'not monsters.' Boff always talked sense. He was so clever he could even spell 'diarrhoea' without looking it up.

'Where do monsters live then?'

'They don't live anywhere,' said the Boff.

6

'Because they don't exist. Except in comics and films.'

'I bet there're loads of monsters in that graveyard,' said Ginger, unimpressed with the Boff's logical approach. 'We should have a look.'

'There's no such thing as monsters…' began the Boff, but Tich cut him off. 'We could still have a look. Nothing else to do is there?'

So they took a diversion into the grounds of St Swithin's, having first checked there was no sign of Daggers. Daggers was the notorious warden at the church whose job amongst other things was to tend the graveyard, which he did with great enthusiasm. He also guarded it from the local vandals who liked to do swastikas in spray paint on the gravestones and kick over the little urns with flowers that people left on the graves.

So, although there were no real monsters in the graveyard, Daggers, who made no distinction between real vandals up to no good and all the other children in the world, could be, in his own way, as scary as any monster, lurking as he did sometimes behind the ash trees waiting to pounce on any children up to unspeakable mischief.

Tich and his gang did not generally get up to unspeakable mischief in the graveyard, unless of course they chanced upon the grave of 'Slasher' Macdonald. 'Slasher' Macdonald was a notorious lunatic who had taught at St Greavsy's school – he'd murdered at least two children by throwing chisels at them, although no one could remember their names or explain why he wasn't sent to jail.

He'd died suddenly of a heart attack. Who could therefore deny Tich and his gang a short dance of joy on his grave and a few kicks at the freshly strewn flowers?

Daggers made no distinction. All children who happened to stray into his territory whether they carried a spray can or not, were the spawn of the devil and should be driven out of the graveyard with sticks at the first opportunity.

Tich and the gang wandered through the graveyard looking at the gravestones and reading the inscriptions. Most of them were old, and old things were rarely interesting despite all the attempts by school teachers to prove otherwise. To Tich, history was a thing of the past and that's where it should be left, forgotten and unstudied forever.

'Over here! Over here!' called Ginger who had found what looked like a little stone house, covered in strange carved figures, in the corner of the graveyard. 'It's Draclea's grave.'

They all rushed over to inspect the plaque on the end of the little stone building. Tich peered closely. 'That doesn't say Dracula, it says "Brian Dricili. Much Loved Butcher and Purveyor of the Finest Black Puddings. 1880 – 1915."'

Ginger read the next line. 'May he rest in peas. Did they used to bury them in peas?'

'Anyway, it's Dricili not Dracula,' said the Boff dismissively.

'Sounds like Draclea,' said Ginger.

'No it doesn't,' said Maggs. 'Doesn't sound anything like Dracula. Sounds more like Piccalilli.'

'It's a funny sort of grave,' said Ginger. 'It's more like a shed.'

'It's called a mausoleum,' explained the Boff. 'They built it to show how important you were.'

'Where's the door?' asked Ginger.

'They don't have doors,' said Maggs. 'It's not as if you're coming in and out, is it? Once you're in there, that's it.'

'Well how did they get him in then?' asked Ginger.

'Maybe they built it around him,' suggested the Boff.

'No, there is an entrance here,' said Maggs pushing against the stone at the end of the mausoleum. It opened a few centimetres and they all jumped back in surprise.

'Look at this.' The Boff was peering intently at the words carved into the stone. 'I think Ginger might be right.'

'Ginger' and 'right' were two words you didn't often hear in the same sentence.

He rubbed the dirt away from the inscription which seemed to say *Dricili*. The lettering was covered in moss which was hiding some of the lines. First the moss fell away from the 'i' and they could now see it was actually an 'a'. The second 'i' was really a 'u' and the final 'i' was really an 'a'.

'Feppin heck! It does say *Dracula*,' said the Boff.

'I told you! I told you it was Draclea,' said Ginger. 'No one ever believes a word what I say.'

'The thing is, though,' said the Boff. 'There never was anyone called Dracula. It was all made up in a book, by a bloke called Bram Stoker. There's no such thing as Dracula. And there's no such thing as vampires. Well, there is vampire bats but they're in South America and they feed on cow's blood. All the rest is just stories.'

'Cow's blood – that's disgusting,' said Ginger. 'Why can't they just drink milk like everyone else?'

Tich stared at Ginger and wondered what it must be like to live in his head.

'I bet Draclea comes out every night,' speculated Ginger.

'You're not listening,'said the Boff. 'You never listen.'

'We should come here, tonight, at midnight and see if he comes out.' Ginger did his best ghost impression, flapping his arms and going 'Woo-woo, Wow-woo.'

'He won't come out, because he's in a book,' said the Boff in irritation.

'You're just chicken,' said Ginger and he started to flap his arms and make chicken noises, 'Bwak-bwark, Bwak-bwark.'

Tich watched Ginger cavorting up and down the path and wished, once again, that his gang didn't consist of such freaks and misfits.

'Even it he doesn't exist, I think we should come here tonight to see what it's like in a graveyard at midnight. Unless, of course, you're all too scared,' said Maggs.

'Nah!' chimed the other three, even though they were scared, but it was important not to admit it, especially to Maggs who was a girl. Well sort of. Besides, things had been a bit boring lately and sneaking out from their homes in the middle of the night did seem like a bit of an adventure.

In a few minutes it was all decided and they set off for home having agreed to meet at the bus shelter opposite the graveyard just as the clock on the church tower struck twelve.

Chapter Two

Nike for Vampires

At home Tich was impatient to get moving. At ten o'clock he stretched his arms theatrically and said, 'Ah well I'm off to bed.'

His mother stared suspiciously. 'You? Bed? Ten o'clock?' Usually going–to-bed-time was a matter of nuclear warfare between Tich and his mum.

Tich would say, 'I've just got to see the end of this programme,' or 'I've just got to finish this Doctor Pepper's,' or 'I've just remembered I've got some homework to do,' were Tich's usual gambits. Sometimes he would also try 'Dad lets me stay up until midnight,' because usually his mum didn't like the idea of being Tich's least popular parent.

This is why Tich's mum was suspicious. 'Are you ill?'

'No, I'm fine. I've just got this good book I'm reading and I've got a maths test at school tomorrow. You know and I'm feeling a bit tired at the moment,' said Tich wondering how many lies he'd need to avert her suspicion.

'Well, no television and no playing the Xbox, if you're tired.'

Darren, who Tich had decided no longer needed to be called Numbskull on the account of the number of times he'd helped Tich out of sticky situations with his mum, winked at him as if he knew all about Tich's plan for the night.

It was a long time until eleven-thirty when Tich planned to set off and he picked up a book that his dad had given him. He read a few lines in the first paragraph but by the time he was half way down the page he was thinking about vampires. Were there really such things? There were loads of films and comics and books about them. There must be some truth in it. He started to read again from the top of the page.

Reading books – how pointless was that?

There was a loud crash as the book hit the

floor. Tich realised he'd fallen asleep. He looked at the clock. It was ten to midnight. He tiptoed to his door, checked all was quiet and then, treading carefully and, avoiding the stair that always creaked, he hurried to the front door, grabbed his coat on the way and, still carrying his shoes, he eased the door open and slipped away into the night. As he stopped on the front path to put his shoes on, the door, which he had so carefully only half-closed behind him, clicked shut and he was locked out, his key left on the dresser by his bed.

He'd worry about that later. It was already two minutes to midnight and he didn't want to be late or, worse still, make the others think he was chicken. He ran through the silent streets which were bathed in yellow light until finally arriving at the bus stop.

'You're late,' accused Maggs.

'I fell asleep,' said Tich.

'We thought you weren't coming,' said the Boff.

'He said you were chicken,' accused Ginger.

'No I didn't,' said the Boff.

He went, 'Bwak-bwark, Bwak-bwark.'

'No I didn't,' countered the Boff.

'Just shut up will you,' said Tich. 'It doesn't matter. We need to get there quick or we might miss him.' Tich led the way through the gate into the churchyard. A little light seeped in from a streetlight casting long dark shadows across the gravestones. There was a light mist that had formed in layers so that the church seemed to be floating on a thin white sea. It swirled as they made their way to the back of the churchyard to the little grey stone mausoleum in the corner.

Maggs and the Boff had brought torches which they shone on moss-mottled stone. They slowly walked around the side where the stone door lay.

'It's moved,' said the Boff

'What?'

'It's moved. Since we looked at it this morning. Look. That gap's nearly two centimetres now. Something's been in there.'

'Or something's come out,' said Ginger.

'Don't be stupid,' said Tich. 'There's only dead people in there.'

Maggs pushed at the stone door and, with

a low grinding sound, it began to open. It was hinged in the middle, so, as one side of the stone moved in, the other moved out. Inside it was pitch black. 'Who's going in first?' asked Ginger.

No one answered. Maggs and the Boff were busying themselves inspecting the outside and pretended not to hear. 'Give us your torch,' said Tich. He took Maggs's torch and shone it inside. He could see cobwebs strung from one side to the other. Huge cobwebs they were and you could be sure with webs that big, the spiders were going to be monsters.

'Who doesn't mind spiders?' asked Tich.

'I don't mind snakes. I held a snake once,' said Ginger.

'Alright,' said Tich wearily. 'Next time we find a place full of snakes we'll know who to send in. Meantime, as there isn't a place full of snakes, WHO ISN'T SCARED OF SPIDERS?'

Even Maggs – fearless against most things – drew the line at spiders. Especially really big ones, in a really dark place that no one had been in for two hundred years. 'We need a stick,' she said.

Tich went over to a bush by the graveyard wall and broke off one of the side shoots. Then, back at the mausoleum, he stuck the stick in ahead of him and waved it about until the worst of the cobwebs were wrapped around it like candy floss. Then he stepped inside.

'It's OK. It's OK,' he said, reassuring himself as much as the others. 'It's empty, sort of. Oh no, hold on, there's a table thing in the middle.' He shone the torch into the centre of the room where there was a stone tomb. Lying on top of the tomb was what looked like a body draped under a thick grey blanket.

The other three entered the mausoleum and joined Tich staring at the tomb.

'Is it stone?' asked Ginger. 'Looks more like an old blanket.'

"Course it's stone,' said the Boff. 'A blanket would have rotted away by now.'

'But do you think that's an actual body under there?' asked Maggs.

'It'd just be ashes and dust by now,' said the Boff. 'OK, we've seen it. It's dead. Let's get out of here.' But as he turned towards the door a huge spider's web broke free and fell against his face enveloping his head and as he tried to tear it off he noticed the biggest spider he'd ever seen crawling over his hand. He flicked it away and it hit the blanket lying on the table.

Their eyes followed the spider as it scuttled across the grey blanket. The blanket started to move. Whatever was under that blanket was sitting up. The four children looked on in horror as the blanket fell away revealing a chalk-white figure with bright red lips and red eyes. It turned its head towards them, opening its black mouth to reveal two blood stained fangs.

'It's Draclea! It's Draclea come to life,' screamed Ginger.

The children were frozen to the spot for a moment and then, realising the figure was turning and lowering its feet to the floor, decided they'd had enough of monsters and vampires and stuff and ran for the door. In their rush, the four of them, jammed into the stone doorway and couldn't push through.

'He's coming. He's coming,' screeched Tich.

The figure behind them was standing now and it began to stumble towards them.

Finally, after a struggle, the children pushed through the door and they tumbled out into the darkness. They jumped to their feet and ran towards the safety of the street lights.

'No such thing as vampires! No such thing as vampires! What was that then?' asked Ginger, a little bit angry for once, and the Boff was, for a change, speechless.

'I can't believe it,' said Maggs

'Believe what?'

'I ran away. I've never run away from anything in my life.'

'It was a vampire,' said Tich. 'If it bit you, you'd become a vampire too. Imagine that: living forever and only coming out at night to drink people's blood. That's worse than being a teacher.'

'What are we going to do?' asked the Boff

'I don't know,' said Tich. 'We'll talk about it tomorrow. Shut your windows tonight though and don't tell anyone.'

They started to go their own ways when Ginger spoke up. 'That vampire,' said Ginger. 'Did anybody else notice it was wearing trainers?'

Chapter Three

From Tomb to Tomb

Twelve hours earlier, while Tich and his gang were inspecting the mausoleum, sitting no more than ten metres away, Pigboy, Barf and Thicko were sharing the last cigarette in the box they had stolen from the newsagent. Pigboy would engage the shopkeeper in interesting conversation while Barf leant over the counter and took a pack or two of their favourite fags.

'It must be brilliant being a newsagent,' Pigboy would say to the man behind the counter. 'I mean, fighting off all them robbers.'

'Well, we don't actually get *that* many robberies. But, you know, you do your best.'

'In fact, I'm thinking of becoming a newsagent when I leave school,' Pigboy would continue. 'Do you have to have a degree in newspapering, or can you like, learn it as you go along?'

The newsagent, unused to hearing of his job in such glowing terms, was more than happy to give this enterprising young boy a brief history of a life that led to the dizzy heights of running his own shop. It was nice for once to meet someone so genuinely interested in him and his undervalued profession

The three boys had been suspended from school for a month. Initially this had seemed a wonderful idea – like an extra summer holiday. Trouble was, with all the other children in school, bullying opportunities were few and far between. Once they had extracted some dinner money from children on their way to school, that was pretty much all the fun they would have for the rest of the day.

They were banned from the Mall and not wanted at home. Their parents had been livid about the school not wanting to see the three of them for a whole month. What were the schools thinking of? It was their job to give them welcome relief from their obnoxious offspring during the day. They shouldn't be sending them home where they'd get up to who knows what.

Eventually their parents compromised and locked them out of their houses during the day. It was much better for them to be out on the street, with a few spray cans and a box of matches, where they couldn't get up to any mischief.

So Pigboy, Barf and Thicko found themselves leaning against the churchyard wall with little to entertain them when suddenly the dark mood was lifted by the sound of voices of children coming from the churchyard. Thicko stood up and peered over the ancient wall.

'Who is it?' asked Barf.

'It's Tich and them lot.'

Pigboy leapt up and pulled Thicko down out of sight. 'Aren't we going to hit them?' asked Thicko disappointedly. For a moment there, the day was beginning to look up. But Pigboy put his finger to his lips to tell him to be quiet and began to listen intently. They were close to the little mausoleum in the corner and managed to hear all the plans for a midnight visit.

After Tich and his gang were safely clear,

Pigboy leapt over the wall and began to inspect the mausoleum. He soon found the stone door which Tich had managed to prise open a little.

Pigboy's mind was awhirl with possibilities. Of course a brutal attack with a few well aimed punches had been an appealing possibility – although they did prefer to attack when Maggs wasn't about, as she often failed to understand the ground rules of bullying and would insists on punching and biting and scratching in a very ungirly-like manner.

But no, Pigboy had resisted the temptation for a little light bullying in favour of a much more devious plan.

'Right,' said Pigboy, 'let's take a look inside.'

As soon as they had noted the layers of cobwebs that had to be pushed aside in order to enter, Barf and Thicko let Pigboy lead the way into the mausoleum. In the centre was what looked like a large stone table but which on inspection was the actual tomb of Mr Brian Dracula, Much Loved Butcher and Purveyor of the Finest Black Puddings.

'What are you doing?' asked Pigboy when he noticed Barf and Thicko were standing back, darting urgent glances as if expecting an attack any second.

'There's spiders in here. Huge hairy spiders,' said Barf. An evil smile played on Pigboy's lips. He looked around and noticed two shining eyes glaring out of the murk, angry at the noisy intrusion to his lair.

Pigboy reached forward and grabbed the spider which was so large that it hardly fitted into his hand. He then leant forward and held his hand directly in front of Barf's face. 'There's nothing to worry about,' he said. 'It's only a little spider,' and with that he opened his hand, releasing the extremely irate spider which leapt for the nearest landing place which happened to be Barf's nose.

Barf screamed which made Thicko scream too and they both bundled out of the mausoleum, leaving Pigboy to exit at his leisure, his mind full of plans for midnight which involved four children, a dusty blanket, some Dracula teeth and a bit of fake blood from the joke shop.

Outside he could hear Thicko and Barf quietly sobbing. Honestly, the day kept getting better and better.

Chapter Four

Tomb it May Concern

At midnight that night, Pigboy's plan had gone like a dream and he was busy dusting himself off, having sent Tich and his gang running away into the night. Barf and Thicko emerged from the shadows and turned on their torch and shone them on the stone door which was now wide open. They waited for Pigboy to emerge, reluctant to enter, knowing that he was likely to jump out on them or throw more spiders.

Inside the mausoleum, Pigboy had turned on his torch and was shining it around the damp grey walls when he noticed that the stone slab he'd been sitting on had moved. It was now at a slight angle to the tomb below.

He touched the slab with his finger and it moved easily as if it had no weight at all.

'Come and look at this,' he said to the others who were still waiting for him outside. Gingerly Barf and Thicko re-entered and stood beside Pigboy. 'This thing moves, look.' He pushed the lid of the tomb. The other two stepped back.

'What's the matter – chicken? Bwak-bwark, Bwak-bwark,' mocked Pigboy. Barf and Thicko stepped forward again torn between fear and humiliation.

Pigboy continued pushing the stone slab until it swung round enough to see inside. Pigboy pointed his torch into the tomb. The other two could hardly bear to look.

'Cool,' said Pigboy, and Thicko and Bark opened their eyes and peered inside.

'It's a skellington,' said Thicko.

'What did you expect – Mr Bean?' said Pigboy scathingly.

'Look. Look at that,' said Barf urgently.

'It's a skeleton. So what?' said Pigboy.

'No, there. Look! Look!'

They peered in closer trying to see what he

was pointing at. Then, with horror, they noticed the large wooden stake sticking out from the skeleton's rib cage. It was placed exactly where the heart would once have been. The others stepped back in shock, but Pigboy was not phased. He leant in and grabbed hold of the stake.

'Don't do that. Don't do that. The skellington will come alive,' said Barf.

'Don't be stupid,' said Pigboy.

He took a firm grasp on the stake and pulled it clear. What he hadn't noticed was a rusty nail in the side of the stake which caught his hand and sent a squirt of blood on to the ribs of the skeleton. The three boys stared in amazement, almost expecting the skeleton to leap up and grab them, but nothing happened.

'I think we should go,' said Barf.

'Yeah alright,' said Pigboy, slightly disappointed he hadn't unleashed a few supernatural creatures. He tossed the stake back into the grave and swung the lid shut. 'Don't want him escaping,' he said and laughed. The other two breathed a sigh of relief as Pigboy left the mausoleum and pushed the stone door closed.

Pigboy reached into his pocket and pulled out his spray can and shook it vigorously. It made that strange clacking sound as the ball-bearing bounced around the tin. 'Shine the torch on the door,' he said and he sprayed on the words 'TICH – CHIKEN. SCARRED OF DRACLEA' and then stood back and admired his handiwork.

The following morning, the Vicar and Daggers stood staring at the ugly red letters on the stone door.

'I blame the schools. You'd think they'd teach them how to spell,' said the Vicar.

'If I catch the kids who did this, I'm going to cut off their heads and impale them on spikes on the churchyard gate. That'd make 'em think,' said Daggers.

'Mmm … Yes … I think beheading might be a little extreme. We are supposed to be Christians after all – turning the other cheek and all that,' said the Vicar.

'Of course. And we will,' replied Daggers. 'Right after I've cut off their arms and legs and rolled their bodies off Pentney Bridge.'

'I knew this would happen,' said the Vicar.

'You can't have a Dracula in your churchyard without some sort of trouble. I thought rubbing that dirt into the inscription might do the trick.'

'They've scraped it all off though. Now everyone can see "Brian Dracula. Much Loved Butcher and Purveyor of the Finest Black Puddings. 1880–1915". We should have just knocked the whole place down and got rid of it once and for all.'

'Leave well alone, that's what I say,' said the Vicar. 'Besides, people'd want to know why we did it. It is a bit of a local feature.'

'You don't want to disturb a vampire, sir,' said Daggers. 'You could end up in all sorts of trouble.'

'Daggers, if I have told you once, I've told you a thousand times – there is no such thing as vampires. Bram Stoker lived around here, you know. I'm sure one day he was strolling through the churchyard and saw the name on that gravestone and thought – "Dracula, hmm, you know that's not a bad name for a vampire. I'll use that in my book". I'm sure there were thousands of perfectly innocent people out there called Mr and Mrs Dracula who were really annoyed with him. They probably had to change their names to stop people following them about with stakes and mallets.'

'There's no smoke without fire, Vicar.'

'Wait a minute,' said the Vicar, who was a bit of an expert on tombs with their doors open. 'I think somebody's opened this tomb. Look, that door isn't shut properly.' He walked over and pushed the stone door. 'Somebody's been in here.'

'I wouldn't go in there if I were you, Vicar,' warned Daggers.

'I'm a Christian, Daggers. I've told you, I do not believe in vampires,' said the Vicar checking the cross around his neck was firmly attached. 'Are you coming? Or are you "scarred of Draclea" too?'

The Vicar pushed open the door and peered inside. 'There's definitely been someone in here. They've cleared all the cobwebs.'

'Just as well,' said Daggers, holding back.

'I suppose the spiders are vampires too, are they? Look, the lid on this tomb has been moved.'

'I shouldn't open that, Vicar. Leave well alone, you said.'

'I'm just going to open it and have a look. I won't have my graves disturbed by vandals.' He pushed the side of the stone slab which swung open so they could see into the tomb.

'What's in there, Vicar?'

'Nothing. Absolutely nothing.'

'Not even a skeleton?'

'Nothing but dust. Although hold on a minute – what's this?' He reached into the coffin and lifted out the pointed wooden stake. 'What on earth is that doing in there?'

Daggers looked at the Vicar and thought to himself, 'Oh no. *Not again.*'

Chapter Five

Headmaster Funk

Mr Grimmell, headteacher at St Greavsy's, was enjoying a quiet drink in his back garden, calculating how many more years he would need to waste his time trying to bring a shaft of light into the dark satanic minds that swarmed into his school each morning.

He had come to call them The Good, the Bad and the Ugly. There was the good – a smattering of hard working children who never swore and went to the library to read books rather than to hide under the bookshelves or set fire to the waste paper baskets.

There were the bad – the bullies, the thieves, the ones who did unspeakable things to the toilets. And then, of course, there were the ugly – the shaven head monsters, who barely qualified as human beings. These could only be restrained temporarily, until they were released into an unsuspecting world where they'd wreak havoc with their spray cans, their junk food litter and only the faintest grasp of the English Language.

Mr Grimmell poured himself another glass of beer. There was a full eighteen hours before he needed to take up the clubs and cudgels and bring the appalling rabble under control for another five and a half tortuous hours.

He watched the sun setting on the horizon and drifted off into a dream of little angels crowded round listening in rapt silence as pearls of wisdoms cascaded from his lips.

The sun had disappeared beneath the horizon and the twilight had just started to fade, when a figure in a black cape and hood appeared lurking amongst the trees at the bottom of the garden.

Stealthily, with barely a sound, it opened the back gate and appeared to drift across the lawn until it stopped directly behind the sleeping headteacher. The hood was discarded to reveal a bleached white head with a few wisps of white hair. The eyes were dark and sunken into their sockets, surrounded by blackened skin. The only colour was the bright red mouth and lips. As the mouth opened, two long razor sharp incisors were revealed.

The creature's head turned as it approached the back of Mr Grimmell's neck and it bared its teeth – teeth so sharp that they could pierce flesh without inflicting the slightest pain.

As the teeth bit into Mr Grimmell's neck, blood spurted out of the two incisions and the Vampire supped greedily while Mr Grimmell dreamed on oblivious.

When the Vampire had drunk its fill, it moved away, staggering slightly, drunk with fresh blood. It slid silently across the lawn swirling the mist around it. Then, in one long movement, it flapped its cloak, which was transformed into two black wings, and it swept into the sky – a dark silhouette against the slow rising moon.

Chapter Six

Doctor What?

The next day, Mr Grimmell was feeling unwell and decided to take a few days off. He was not feeling any better by the middle of the week so he set off to visit the doctor. He found the light in the street so bright he was forced to return home and fetch his sunglasses. As he sat in the waiting room, Mr Grimmell noticed that all the other patients were wearing dark glasses, even though it was cloudy and dark outside.

After a short wait, he went in and began explaining his symptoms to the doctor.

'When I'm outside during the day, I find the light very bright, even if it's cloudy and I feel very, very hungry all the time, but I find normal food strangely unsatisfying – except Black Pudding. In fact I could eat Black Puddings all day.'

The doctor looked at him over his glasses. 'A

strong desire to eat Black Pudding is not really a symptom of anything,' he said. 'Apart from greed,' he added.

'Yes, but there's more. I was just going to take a bite of my garlic bread last night and I found it strangely revolting. I had to put it straight in the bin.'

'Perhaps it'd gone off.'

'And I can't sleep at night. I just feel like throwing myself out of the window and flying away into the night.'

'You mustn't do that,' said the doctor, alarmed. 'That can be very dangerous. Unless you live in a bungalow. Do you live in a bungalow?'

'No.'

'Then you definitely mustn't throw yourself out of the window. We can't have people throwing themselves out of windows willy-nilly. There could be some very nasty injuries.'

'Also I've noticed cats and other things hissing at me and arching their backs.'

'What other things?'

'Well, just cats mainly.' Mr Grimmell paused. 'Also, I called in at the church but I couldn't walk through the door. It's as if there was a massive force field keeping me out.'

'Massive force field, you say,' repeated the doctor who had started typing all the symptoms into his laptop.

'And I'm having this problem when I have a shave in the morning. I keep cutting myself. There seems to be some sort of problem with my reflection.'

'Problem?'

'I don't seem to have one.'

'No reflections in the mirror,' the doctor said, as he typed, pretending to be interested but getting a bit bored now with so many symptoms.

'And I'm having some, you know, some marital problems.'

'Really,' said the doctor, perking up, wondering if he was going to hear something saucy.

'Yes,' said Mr Grimmell. 'You see, my wife likes to sleep horizontally on the bed, but these days, I prefer to, sort of, hang from the ceiling. I wrap my feet around the lightshade and just sort of, hang there.'

'You do realise hanging from the ceiling can

be very dangerous. Many serious injuries are caused by people hanging upside down from lightshades,' warned the doctor. 'I know about these things. I'm a doctor, you know.'

'Yes. Yes. I know. But hanging upside down is the only way I can get to sleep.'

'I see. That's the lot is it? All the symptoms?' asked the doctor.

'Yes.'

'Right. Let me have a think about this.' The doctor pressed ENTER on his laptop and pretended to think. What he was actually doing though, was waiting for his laptop to process all the symptoms and tell him what was wrong with Mr Grimmell.

Suddenly the answer came back. It was a huge red word flashing across the whole screen. The laptop started making alarm noises: 'Dee Dah Dee Dah Dee Dah' like an ambulance with its siren on.

The doctor slammed the laptop shut. But the alarm kept sounding 'Dee Dah Dee Dah Dee Dah'. He yanked the laptop lead out of the socket, but still the noise continued.

He opened a drawer in his desk, put the

laptop in it and slammed the drawer shut but, even then, you could still hear the strangulated wail of the laptop alarm.

'Is something the matter?' Mr Grimmell asked.

'No. No, nothing at all. That's computers for you. Got a bit of a bug I expect. Worse than humans,' he said and laughed unconvincingly.

'So what's the verdict, Doctor, now you've had time to think about it?'

'Well, there's nothing serious Mr Grimmell. I think you'll find it'll all sort itself out in a couple of days.'

'Nothing wrong then?'

'No, probably just a touch of Hong Kong flu.'

'But I don't have any flu symptoms.'

'Ah yes, but this is Hong Kong flu – entirely different thing. Hong Kong flu makes you sensitivity to light, dislike garlic and hang upside down to sleep.'

'What about the church?'

'Aversion to churches. That's another symptom. Nothing to worry about. Perfectly normal if you've caught Hong Kong Flu.'

The doctor opened the drawer which contained hundreds of little bottles which he kept for emergencies and for patients who wouldn't go away easily.

'I tell you what. Take one of these pills every day and you'll soon be feeling better.'

'They look a bit like Smarties,' said Mr Grimmell.

'Yes, they do, don't they. All those colours. But they're not. They're definitely really good illness pills for Hong Kong flu. They'll soon have you right as rain.'

Mr Grimmell left the doctor's feeling strangely unsatisfied. At the back of his mind he couldn't help feeling that something really was the matter with him. He felt the same when he went back to school the next day and prepared to address the children in assembly. As he looked out at the sea of expectant faces he noticed at least half of the pupils had, like him, taken to wearing dark glasses.

Chapter Seven

Invasion of the Body Poppers

'There's something funny going on,' announced Tich. He had called an emergency meeting of the gang to discuss the latest developments.

'Like what?' asked Ginger.

'For one thing,' said Tich. 'In assembly this morning half the people were wearing dark glasses.'

'What's wrong with that. It was sunny,' said Ginger.

'It was in the hall and the curtains were closed. And you're not allowed to wear dark glasses. It's in the school rules.'

'Mr Grimmell's been wearing them for weeks.'

'Exactly. He never wears glasses.'

'And another thing,' said Tich. 'Why have they taken all the mirrors down from the loos?'

'Perhaps they've gone to be repaired,' said Maggs.

'All of them? All at once?'

'I noticed something,' said the Boff. 'All the people wearing sun glasses only drink Ribena at lunchtime. I tried some and it tasted disgusting. It was thick, like a milk shake. And they're always yawning in class. It's like they've been up all night. And nobody says anything.'

'Maybe ...' commenced Ginger. 'Maybe ... '

'What?'

'I don't want to say ... You'll all laugh at me,' said Ginger.

''Course we won't,' said the others, all getting ready to have a good laugh. It was Ginger. It was bound to be something dumb.

'Maybe they've all turned into vampires.'

The other three hesitated. It was, of course, a stupid suggestion. On the other hand, with such weird things going on, they were pretty much ready to believe even the most ridiculous possibility.

'What do we know about vampires?' asked Tich.

'They can turn into bats.'

'They drink blood.'

'You have to shoot them with a silver bullet,' suggested Ginger.

'That's werewolves, not vampires, you tonk,' said the Boff.

'They don't like garlic or crosses. An', if they bite you, you turn into a vampire too.'

'They don't have a reflection in the mirror,' said Maggs.

'That's why they took the mirrors away. Maybe Ginger's right.'

It had never occurred to them that Ginger could be right about anything, but maybe on this occasion …

'We need to do an experiment,' said the Boff. 'To find out once and for all.' He paused. 'So – who can we do an experiment on?' The children looked at each other and then in one voice called out, 'Barky.'

Barky lived three doors up from Tich in a very scruffy house with several wrecks of cars and a caravan on the front lawn. Barky wore clothes from Oxfam and it was generally agreed that it was best to stay upwind of him, as he often gave off some very unusual smells.

One day he came to school smelling strongly of wood smoke and the fire brigade had been called before the teachers had identified Barky as the source of the pungent aroma.

Ginger was dispatched to collect Barky. Tich knew he would come immediately because he didn't have any friends. He'd be seated as usual, at the front window of the caravan, desperately hoping that someone would come round to ask him out to play. An invitation that, until this day, had sadly never come.

Chapter Eight

Barky Loner

Ten minutes later Barky was sitting on the carpet in Tich's bedroom. 'Can I be in your gang now?' asked Barky hopefully.

'Yeah maybe,' replied Tich, allowing this blatant lie to hang in the air for a while until all experiments had been completed and Barky could be safely dispatched home.

Tich, Maggs, the Boff and Ginger inspected the urchin before them. There was, as usual, a fairly pungent smell emanating from Barky, and, as usual, it was difficult to pinpoint what it actually was. There was a touch of burning car tyre here, a touch of boiling cabbage there, a smattering of wet dog and a top note of the faintest suggestion of rancid chip fat.

'People who want to be in our gang have to pass some tests,' lied Maggs.

'I'm ready,' said Barky wiping his runny nose on his sleeve. If he'd been a dog, his tail would have been wagging furiously by now.

'Why have you started wearing sunglasses?' asked the Boff.

'I don't know,' said Barky. 'It's the light. It hurts my eyes.'

'Would you like a slice of garlic bread?' Tich offered a slice he'd borrowed from the fridge.

'Yes, please,' said Barky, although he hated garlic bread. He went to grab the slice from the plate but, as he reached over, suddenly his arm flew back as if he'd just touched an electric wire.

'Maybe not,' he said. 'I'm not all that hungry.'

'What do you think of this?' said Maggs, holding out the tiny crucifix she wore on a chain around her neck.

'S'alright,' said Barky cautiously.

'Would you like to wear it?' asked Maggs, lifting the necklace over her head and advancing on Barky.

'No, no,' said Barky leaping backwards. 'I don't like them.'

'You said you did.'

'Well, I don't. And I think your tests are stupid.'

'You want to be in our gang, don't you?'

'Yes.'

'Well, you have to do the tests then.'

'Shall we push him out of the window and see if he flies off,' whispered Maggs to Tich.

'You're not pushing me out of the window,' said Barky, overhearing.

'No. I know,' said the Boff. 'Come into the bathroom, Barky.'

'I'm not havin' a wash,' said Barky. 'I'm allergic to soap.'

'Yeah, we did notice,' said Tich.

The Boff led the way into the bathroom and all five of them trooped in. The Boff nodded towards the mirror over the sink. In the reflection there were only four children. There was no sign of Barky.

'Let's have a look at your neck,' said Maggs and Barky lifted his head. It was difficult to see much on Bark's neck, layers of dirt having built up over the years. They all peered closer. There in the greyness were two dark red circles with a dried blood caked around them. There was no doubt about it. Barky had been bitten by a vampire.

They all walked back into Tich's room in silence.

'Can I be in you gang now?' asked Barky plaintively.

'Of course you can't,' said Tich. 'You've failed all the tests. 'You'd better go home now.' Barky's face fell in disappointment.

'I didn't like your tests anyway. They were rubbish,' said Barky defiantly, although he couldn't quite hide the tremor in his voice. He walked out of the room, suppressing a tear, his shoulders hunched.

'Just a minute,' said Tich. Barky's face lit up. They'd changed their minds. At last, at last he was going to have some friends.

'You forgot these,' said Ginger, handing him his sunglasses. Barky took the glasses and walked out of the house and along the path, kicking the ground disconsolately as he went. Maybe tomorrow someone would really want him in their gang. Then he'd show 'em.

'This is serious,' said Tich. 'Half the school

has already turned into vampires. We're in deep do do.'

'We'd better not go into school any more,' said the Boff.

The three friends nodded their heads in agreement.

Tich mulled it over and, after some thought, said, 'No. It's no good telling my mum I can't go to school anymore 'cause I might get bitten by a vampire. She'd never believe me. Last week I told her there was an outbreak of Ebola virus and she still made me to go. Ebola makes your blood boil and your head explode. What sort of mother sends a kid to school when his head might explode?'

'No,' he continued, 'I need to speak to my dad about vampires. He's bound to know all about them. He knows everything.' Tich didn't add 'although nothing about anything useful,' which was usually the case with his dad's advice. 'But we've all got to be careful. No going out at night and we should all wear polo neck sweaters so they can't get you in the neck.'

Chapter Nine

Fangs for Nothing

Tich had sent everybody home with a warning to be careful. A few moments later he left the house on his way to his dad's flat. He'd just turned into the alleyway, when he saw Abigail Mountford approaching from the other direction.

He was determined not to look at her because, if their eyes met, Tich knew his face would take on the colour of a cooked beetroot and she would giggle at him and he'd wish he could disappear between the cracks in the paving stones.

Of all his ambitions – playing football for England, winning the British Grand Prix at the age of fifteen – only one stood above all others and that was a date with Abigail Mountford.

He looked down at the ground – always

a good strategy in that alley way anyway to avoid that squelch underfoot that told you a dog had been that way not long before.

She was only a few steps away now – a few more moments and he'd be safe. He might even risk a backwards glance to drink in the sight of her blonde hair flowing in the breeze.

'Hello, Tich.' He couldn't believe it. She'd spoken his name. She actually knew his name!

'Where are you going, Tich?'

'My dad's,' he said.

'What are you going to do there?'

'Home ...' he just stopped himself in time from saying 'Homework' which might just have been the uncoolest thing any human being could possibly say at a moment like this. He changed tack. 'Just going to hang out, you know, play games and stuff.'

So far, so good. He'd managed to get this far without burbling like a lunatic.

'Can I come with you?'

Tich stared in incomprehension. This was Abigail Mountford. Abigail Mountford who looked about eighteen with blonde hair and blue eyes and was as close to a Barbie Doll as was humanly possible. Not only was she speaking to him, but she was offering to come to his dad's with him.

Her face was very close now. 'Do you like me, Tich?'

'Yeah, yeah, you know, a bit.'

'Would you like me to kiss you?'

Fireworks filled the sky and heavenly choirs sang Hallelujah. Tich's feet lifted off the ground. Thank you. Thank you God and from now on I will always say the proper words to the Lord's Prayer and not:

Our farmer who farts in Devon

Harold be thy name.

'Close your eyes.'

Tich did as he was told. He was now under celestial control.

'You don't need to screw them up like that. You look like a loony. Just close them.' Tich tried to relax his face.

'That's it. That's much better.'

There was a pause as she moved her face towards Tich's. Tich wanted to open his eyes but didn't dare. He could feel her breath on his face as her lips drew closer. Her breath smelt of rotting flesh which wasn't quite how he'd imagined it. Still.

But unseen to Tich, her face passed his and she drew her lips back to reveal two blood-stained incisors plunging hungrily down towards Tich's neck.

Suddenly, there was an abominable scream and, like a fur-ball spat out of the mouth of hell, a small hairy object came flying towards Tich and Abigail. It was Maggs, soaring through the air, feet first, knocking Abigail clean off her feet with a two-legged karate kick, smashing her against the fence where she collapsed onto the tarmac screeching and hissing violently.

Tich, transfixed by the kiss that was never to come, finally had to open his eyes only to see Abigail running away down the alley and Maggs slapping her hands together after a job well done.

'What have you done, you tonk?' screamed Tich taking in the scene in horrified disbelief. 'I was just going to kiss Abigail Mountford. Now you've scared her away.'

'She's a vampire,' said Maggs firmly.

'No she isn't. She can't be. She's too beautiful,' argued Tich.

'Anyway. Why would she want to kiss *you*? – Yecch.'

Slowly the truth dawned on Tich. She was right. Maggs had just saved him from a vampire. 'She was going to kiss me,' he said sadly.

'She was going to tear your throat out.'

'I knew that,' said Tich. 'I was going to trap her.'

'Yeah, 'course you were,' said Maggs.

Chapter Ten

A History of Short Vampires

Tich banged on the door of his father's flat.

'It's open. Come on in.'

Tich walked through the dusty book-strewn living room and into the kitchen, which smelled of old cabbage and fish. The table was covered as usual in old dishes and unwashed cups. 'Sorry about the mess,' said his dad. 'I usually clear up on Wednesdays. Didn't get round to it this week. Do you want a drink?'

Tich looked at the green mould growing out of one of the mugs. 'Probably not at the moment thanks.'

'Your mother rang earlier. Said you're in trouble at school again.'

'She's stupid.'

'You shouldn't really talk about your mother like that.'

'She won't listen.'

'Yes, well. Listening's never been her strong point. So. What's the problem this time?'

'It's the vampires.'

'Vampires?'

'Nearly the whole school has turned into vampires. That's why I can't go back. If I do they'll bite me on the neck and I'll be a vampire too. I'll live forever and only come out at night to drink people's blood.'

'Well I heard some excuses for not going to school, but I think that's probably the best one yet.'

'I'm not joking.'

'It is vampires we're talking about. They don't actually exist, Tich. They're a myth. The idea's been around for thousands of years, but there was this book called *Dracula* by Bram Stoker ... '

Tich had a feeling books were going to come into this somewhere.

'There've been all these books and films based on that novel. That's where it's all come from. It's all fiction.'

'But you said the idea's been around for thousands of years.'

'Versions of it, yes. The Celts used to put heavy stones on the graves to stop people coming back. Sometimes when graves got opened they found some very strange things. Sometimes corpses blow up like balloons and when people saw them they thought the corpses'd been out gorging themselves on blood.'

'Eeeuuw. Gross,' said Tich.

'Also, sometimes they buried people when they weren't actually dead. They heard them banging on the box and people thought they were vampires trying to get out. Sometimes they'd open a coffin and bang a stake in the heart to make sure they were really dead.'

'Why would they bury them if they weren't dead?'

'Because, in those days, people didn't know how to tell if someone was dead or not. They didn't know about comas and things like that. The truth is, it's not very nice all this – what happens to people when they die. And it gives people strange ideas. Or it did.

'People don't believe this stuff any more. We know what happens to people when they die now and we know when they're really dead. We understand things better. That's why we don't believe in vampires anymore.'

'I don't believe in vampires. At least I didn't, until people started to come to school in sunglasses. And Abigail Mountford tried to bite my neck. And Barky had teeth marks on his neck. I'm not lying to you, Dad.'

Tich's dad stared at him for a long time before he spoke. 'You've never lied to me, Tich. I know you don't lie.' He paused. 'I just think there has to be another explanation for what's going on. Have you heard of an illness called porphyria?'

'No.'

'It makes your teeth stick out. It makes you sensitive to light and makes you hate garlic. It even makes your teeth and bones fluorescent. They used to think drinking blood was a cure for it. Maybe it's like a virus. Maybe that's what's happening.'

'Even if it is, it doesn't help,' said Tich. 'We've still got to deal with it.'

Tich's father had stood up and was looking along his shelves. He chose a big book and handed it to Tich. 'This might give you some ideas.' He handed his son a copy of the *The Boys' Big Book of Vampires* by Peter Haining. Tich marvelled at the way that his father could always produce a book whatever the subject.

If only books were of any use.

Chapter Eleven

Mum's the Word

On Monday morning Tich was sitting at the breakfast table with his mum and Darren. Tich used to call Darren 'Numbskull' but he'd stopped when he realised that Darren was often on his side – in a careful sort of way – in arguments with his mum. And when arguing with his mum you needed all the allies you could get.

It was Darren who'd opened the door when Tich'd come back from the graveyard in the middle of the night, because Tich was sure the door had shut behind him when he left. Darren had a funny way of knowing what was going on and helping out.

'I can't go to school today.'

'W'as up? Aren't you well?' asked Darren, winking.

'I've got this terrible stomach ache.' Tich

had found that a terrible stomach was the best illness to make up because unlike tonsillitis or flu there was no outward sign of the disease to give the game away. All that was required was a pained look on the face. Unfortunately his mum was growing wise to Tich's game.

'Well, you ate your breakfast quick enough. You can't have *that* much of a tummy ache.'

Tich inwardly cursed himself for such an elementary mistake. What he should have done was to take one mouthful of breakfast, push the plate away and then put his hand on his tummy and say in a pathetic sort of voice, 'I can't eat this. Sorry. I'd better get off to school.'

Then he should have waited until his mum said, 'Are you feeling ill, Kevin?'

Then he should have said, 'Don't worry I'll probably be alright for school. I could always go to the sick room if the pain gets too much.'

He would then have had the day off and an Oscar for the best feigned illness performance of the year. Instead he'd blundered in with his 'tummy ache' thing and now he could only try and recover with something different.

'I haven't really got a stomach ache. I'm just

frightened to go to school. I'm being bullied. There's this big boy keeps stealing my money and punching me.'

'What his name?' asked his mum. Tich cursed himself again. He hadn't prepared his brief sufficiently and the council for the prosecution was cutting through his defence like a baseball bat through a 99p candy floss. Tich snatched a name out of the air.

'Barky. His name's Barky.'

It was a long shot. As long as his mum didn't know that Barky was a three-foot dwarf who smelled like an Oxfam Shop, he'd be alright.

'Barky! That's the boy down the street, isn't it? You're not frightened of *him* are you. I could knock him over with a matchstick.'

Tich had only one more chance – the truth. Always a last resort but it very occasionally did the trick.

'Alright. I can't go to school today because half the people there have turned into vampires. Even the teachers. If I go to school, they'll make me one of them and I'll be forced to walk the earth as the undead, sucking blood out of people for eternity.'

'Vampires, again. I've never heard such nonsense,' said his mother. 'Vampires, for goodness' sake, can't you come up with something more convincing than that?'

'Dad believed me,' insisted Tich. Ooops, bad move, he thought. Never ever mention his dad in a disagreement with his mum.

'Well of course, he would, wouldn't he? Your father lives in a world of his own. All those books. It's not normal, you know, having all those books lying around. No wonder he's always filling your head with such nonsense. Now,' she said decisively, 'you haven't got a tummy ache, you're not being bullied and no one is going to turn you into a vampire. So pick up that backpack to get yourself off to school.'

'Fine,' said Tich. 'I'll go and don't blame me if the next time you see me I'll be lying in a coffin with a big stake through my heart.'

What's the point of parents? Tich thought to himself as he joined the flow of small bodies on their way to school. I bet if social services got to know about my mum I'd have to be taken into care. Where was the justice in it all?

Chapter Twelve

Bats Entertainment

An hour later, the children were seated in the hall listening to one of Mr Grimmell's increasingly weird assemblies. Tich had noticed that instead of dreaming of crisps, or counting the wall bars, or listening for accidental farts, or winking at your mates, or all the usual things that people did to survive one of Mr Grimmell's interminable assemblies, the children with sunglasses had taken to hanging on his every word, as if it was possible he might be saying something that was actually worth listening to.

They all sat bolt upright, didn't fidget, or yawn. They just sat there, row upon row of sunglassed heads, drinking in Grimmell's every word, making Tich and the gang feel like they had stumbled into the company of a weird cult, like the Mormons, or the Boy Scouts, or Jehovah's Witlesses, or something like that.

Today's subject, it seemed, was the General Wonderfulness of Bats. 'Many ignorant people,' said Mr Grimmell, 'believe bats are ugly creatures, like mice or rats, flying through the darkness just waiting to get entangled in someone's hair. Nothing could be further from the truth. Imagine, if you will, flying through the air at night, light as a feather, wheeling and diving, swooping and looping with your radar pings mapping an aural landscape ahead of you.'

'Ain't that the truth!' called out one of the teachers.

'Now some people say – what about those vampire bats? Superstitious nonsense I say. Why sup blood when the air is so full of delicious insects and creepy crawlies to devour? People shouldn't be complaining, they should be thanking us ... er .... bats I mean ... for clearing the air and making it safe for people to breathe at their leisure.'

Suddenly Mrs Wilson's eyes glazed over

and she leapt out of her seat and screamed, 'Draculula, Draculula.' Then she noticed all eyes were on her, and she sat down sheepishly on her seat, her face glowing red.

The Boff's hand shot up. Mr Grimmell eyed him suspiciously. Tich nudged him violently and muttered, 'Shut up.'

'Yes Pravin, have you got something to tell us?'

'There *is* such a thing as vampire bats. They live in South America. They drink the blood of cattle and spread rabies.'

Mr Grimmell glared at Pravin. 'Thank you for that information, Pravin. It just happens, on this occasion, you are mistaken.'

'No I'm not,' Pravin began to say, but Tich put his arm around his head and his hand across his mouth.

'You see Pravin, even Kevin agrees with me.'

'My friends,' he continued. 'We have nothing to fear from the common bat – it is time instead to applaud him, to open our arms and welcome him as a fellow creature. Let us join together and praise the wonderful bat, our protector and vigilante of the night.'

And with that the whole hall leapt up and formed a conga line, kicking their feet up in the air and singing:

'We're all going Vampire.

We're all going Vampire.

Der Der, da da, der der, da da.

Der Der, da da, der der, da da.'

Only four people failed to join the joyous throng. Tich and the gang remained seated in the centre of the hall, their arms folded and with dark frowns on their faces. The slow realisation dawned – the entire school had gone stark staring bonkers.

Children were actually cheering one of Mr Grimmell's assemblies – what was next? – flying pigs, cars made of cardboard, talking biscuits?

'Please be seated.' The crowd in the gym quietened and sat down. Tich noticed that there were no more gaps in the sunglasses. With the exception of Tich and his gang, every single pupil and every single teacher was wearing dark glasses.

'It occurs to me,' said Mr Grimmell, 'that there may be some among us who are less keen on the beautiful bat than others. Some who prefer to go their own way despite the clear superiority of bats to all other living creatures. Well, everyone is entitled to their opinion, however misguided that may be.'

Five hundred pairs of eyes turned on Tich and his gang.

'That is all for this morning. There will be a prize at the end of the week for the best topic book on the subject of *The Excellence of Bats*. The prize will be this lovely bottle of Ribena.' He held up the bottle of red liquid and winked at his audience. 'Right, now back to your roosts, I mean, to your classrooms.'

Chapter Thirteen
Night Nurse

As the children began to leave the hall, Mr Grimmell called out, 'Oh, and by the way, I'd like to see these four people in my study right away: Maggie Harvey, Charles Bizley, Pravin Patel and Kevin Smith.'

The other children continued filing out while Tich and his gang stood staring disconsolately on the floor. 'You should have kept your mouth shut, Pravin,' said Tich to the Boff.

'But he's talking rubbish.'

'He's always talking rubbish, so why did you have to stick your hand up *now*?'

'Are they going to turn us into vampires?' asked Ginger.

'Not if I can help it,' said Maggs. 'If they try it with me I'll punch their stupid spikey teeth out.'

'There's hundreds of them. We can't fight all of them,' said the Boff.

'We have to be careful,' said Tich. 'We just need to stick together. If we do that, they can't get us.'

'But what if the whole world turns into vampires?' asked Ginger and, for once, they didn't tut or make faces.

Tich said, 'If the whole school's become vampires in a week, how long before the whole country are vampires?'

They made their way slowly and reluctantly towards Mr Grimmell's office. This was a bad enough journey at the best of times, when they would be expecting a telling off. But right now, they might be headed for certain death, or maybe something even worse.

Tich knocked on the door. 'Come in,' said Grimmell brightly. 'Ah, welcome, welcome,' he said, as the four children eyed him suspiciously. 'Step forward. No need to look so down in the mouth. It's not the end of the world, is it? Have a toffee.'

'Have a toffee! Have a toffee!' Grimmell giving out toffees? Now we know he really is mad, thought Tich. Grimmell had never offered anyone a toffee in the whole of his life.

'Go ahead, take one,' he insisted. 'We're all friends here.'

'Friends!' thought Tich. 'Headmasters don't have friends.'

'They're a funny colour,' said Pravin. 'They're red. They look like …'

'Like what?'

'Like clotted blood.'

'Ha ha, you're so funny, Pravin,' said Mr Grimmell tousling Pravin's hair. 'I've gone off toffees myself. They get stuck round my teeth.' He pointed at his teeth and Tich could see the glint of those sharp incisors just hidden from view. 'Now children, the thing is that I've heard a rumour that some children in the school are suffering from nits.'

'Nits. Aren't they the things that fly about at night and suck out all your blood,' asked Tich innocently.

'No, no. I think you're getting confused, Kevin. They're perfectly harmless, but we must check for them, as they do tend to spread rather quickly. Step into my office, please.'

'Ladies,' he called out, and four identical plump ladies, all wearing nurses' uniforms and sunglasses, joined them in the room.

'Now these nice ladies are nurses and they're just going to check that you don't have head lice in your hair. Nothing to be afraid of.'

The four ladies lined up, one behind each child. 'Now just stand perfectly still and it'll all be over in a second.' Each of the four plump ladies leaned forward and, at the last minute, opened their mouths wide to reveal the razor sharp teeth which honed in on four, slightly grubby, necks.

'They're vampires. Run for it,' shouted Tich rushing for the door. But Mr Grimmell was too quick and he placed himself between the children and the door. The nit nurses were running round the desk to catch them. Maggs got to the window and threw back the blind. 'Grab their glasses.'

The others snatched the sunglasses off the nit nurses' noses. The nurses screamed and shielded their eyes, temporarily blinded by the light, allowing the children just enough time to jump out of the window and race across the tarmac.

'They're getting away. They're getting away,' shouted Mr Grimmell, running along the corridor flinging the classroom doors open as he went. Soon streams of children were pouring out of the classrooms, out of the building and into the playground in hot pursuit of Tich and his gang. 'Catch them and bring them back to me,' called out Mr Grimmell. 'And we shall all feast on fresh blood tonight.'

'Unusual sort of activity,' said a voice behind Mr Grimmell. Mr Grimmell turned to see Watkins the school inspector who'd arrived on a surprise visit.

'Yes, yes,' said Mr Grimmell, thinking quickly. 'It's part of our comparative religions module. Come inside,' he said, putting his arm round Watkins's shoulders. 'And I'll show you our aims and objectives.'

Chapter Fourteen

Fly Me To The Goons

Tich and his gang ran as fast as they could out of the school gate, along the road and into the alley leading to the canal. A couple of hundred metres behind came five hundred children in sunglasses shouting, 'Blood. We must have blood.'

Two pensioners were just leaving their front gate when they found themselves buffeted by an unruly gang of razor-toothed children. When the throng had finally passed them, one said, 'When I was at school we used to go on Nature Walks.'

'That's the problem with youngsters these days,' said the other, 'they're all turning into feppin vampires.'

Meanwhile the chase was on. The four friends had turned the corner and were now running along the towpath alongside the canal. When the raging throng emerged from the alleyway, the leaders looked up and down the path trying to spot the fugitives.

This moment's hesitation caused a bottleneck and the children, pushing through from behind, caused the leaders to be shoved over the edge into the canal. Dozens of children fell into the shallow, stagnant water. They hissed and wailed and squealed – water is like acid to a vampire.

Taking advantage of this temporary halt, the four friends turned to look back briefly and then to run on round the corner out of sight where they could lose themselves in the old warehouses.

Such was the plan, but what they hadn't bargained for was the three figures currently lounging on the broken bench ahead. It was Pigboy and his two partners-in-crime, Thicko and Barf, still suspended from school.

They were bored, the three of them – there were no small children to terrify, no lunch boxes to be plundered, no mobile phones to be torn from the hands of pretty girls pining for handsome young boy bands, and no teachers to annoy from the back of the class.

In short, life had become rather tame, so the sight of the Tich and his friends roaring round the corner promised welcome relief. They roused themselves from their stupor, stubbed out their fags and positioned themselves across the path so there was no way through.

Tich and his friends stopped themselves just in time and then hesitated, sizing up the situation. Ahead were the Goons – the three most feared bullies in the town. Behind were five hundred blood-crazed vampires who, at this moment, were overcoming their confusion and about to resume the chase with renewed vigour.

'What do we do?' asked the Boff.

'We could swim for it,' suggested Ginger.

'You can't swim in the canal, there's hardly any water and it's full of shopping trolleys,' said Tich. 'You'd die of pollution.'

'We should stand and fight 'em. Smash in their faces,' suggested Maggs.

'There's five hundred of them,' said Tich.

'Five hundred and three, if you count the Goons,' corrected the Boff.

'We can't fight five hundred kids. We've got to keep going forward,' said Tich. He strode forward and addressed Pigboy. 'Any minute now,' he said, 'there's five hundred vampires coming round this corner.'

'Five hundred, less the ones in the canal,' corrected the Boff.

'They don't need to know that, you wazzock,' said Tich through his teeth.

'Oh yeah,' said Pigboy. 'Five hundred vampires. What to do you think I am, stupid?'

'Yeah. Pull the other one,' said Thicko. 'It's got bells on it.' The three Goons roared with laughter at Thicko's dazzling wit.

'Get out of our way,' fumed Maggs, bored with the talk and spoiling for a fight.

'OK,' said Tich to his friends. 'Let's go for it,' and with that the four of them, with Maggs to the fore, charged at the Goons. This resolute action caught the Goons off guard. They had no time to brace themselves as the four friends barged into them at full pelt. Barf and Thicko fell to the ground, but Pigboy, with many pounds of flesh anchoring him to the ground, was only briefly knocked sideways

'Get up. Get up,' he shouted at Barf and Thicko. 'They're not getting away with that. I'm going to beat the living daylights out of them.'

Barf and Thicko jumped up and brushed themselves down and they were about to begin the chase, when Barf stopped and said, 'What's that noise?'

They listened. There was a weird wailing sound like a thousands cats screeching in the night. Seconds later, as Tich had predicted, five hundred vampires came charging around the corner, baying for blood.

For a second, the Goons were rooted to the spot, unable to move through surprise and sheer terror – an emotion, it must be said, of which they had little experience. They were used to dealing out fear, less familiar with dealing with it themselves.

'Run for it', shouted Pigboy and they took off down the towpath.

'Where to?'

'Just follow Tich.'

If there were any justice in the world, the sight of the Goons, firstly being knocked about by Tich and his gang and then pursued by every other child in the school, might be seen to be justice finally done. The three boys whose bullying had terrorized an entire school were finally getting their just desserts but, as with everything else, the arrival of the vampires had turned the world on its head.

The Goons had merely inflicted minor bruising and the loss of the occasional Snickers bar. The vampires wanted to bite your neck and suck out your soul leaving you doomed to wander eternally as the Undead searching for new victims. Beside them, Pigboy and the Goons were quite sweet really.

Chapter Fifteen

Semi Attacked

The Goons, despite their nicotine habit, were soon running along beside Tich and the gang.

'Where are we going?'

'We?' thought Tich. 'What does he mean *we*?'

'Tich's is nearest,' said Ginger and the seven of them ran off in that direction. They dashed across the road, opened the front gate and ran up to the door.

Meanwhile the vampire children flooded out of the alleyway and spilled out across the road. So strong was their blood lust that they didn't notice the sleek sports car roaring towards them.

In the car, a sporting goods salesman was driving at 45mph in a 30mph limit. He was allowed to do this because his reactions were much quicker than an ordinary driver and he therefore did not need speed limits to drive safely.

On this occasion though, as he rounded the corner to find the road full of little vampires, even his panther-like reactions were not quick enough to prevent him crashing into the crowd and knocking over twenty-five children.

As the salesman later pointed out, this was entirely the fault of the children who had not crossed the road with sufficient caution as they were too busy salivating, shouting 'Blood, blood. Give us blood.' And so on.

The salesman might have felt worse about knocking the children down if they hadn't almost immediately jumped up, clicked their little arms and legs into place, shaken off the excess blood and resumed their pursuit.

Tich and the others had heard the screech of tyres and were looking back. 'Did you see that,' said Pigboy. 'He knocked them down and they just got up again. You can't kill them.'

Once they'd reached Tich's house, Tich open the door, let the others in and slammed the door behind them. A voice called out from the living room: 'You're home early, Kevin. Everything all right?'

'Fine, Mum.'

Tich led the others upstairs. They looked out of the window and saw hundreds of little figures swarming around the front of the house, each little face distorted in hatred, eyes burning with fire and blood-stained fangs barely concealed by blood red lips. They swarmed round beside the side of the house and filled the garden at the back, trapping the fugitives. They began banging frantically on the doors and windows.

As soon as they spotted Tich looking out of the window, the cry went up. 'They're here. They're here. Kill them! Kill them! Suck their blood until their veins run dry.'

A voice called up from downstairs. 'Kevin can you tell your friends to be quiet, we're trying to watch the television. There's a programme about wallpaper we're trying to watch. It's very interesting.'

'What's going on? What's happened to them kids?' demanded Pigboy.

'The Vampire escaped from that grave place.

It's started biting people and turning them into vampires,' explained Ginger.

'Don't be daft,' said Pigboy. 'That wasn't vampires, that was just us messing about.'

'The whole school has turned into vampires – even the dinner ladies,' continued Ginger. 'We're the only ones left – and you – 'cause you're not at school.'

'That's because we don't wanna be at school,' said Barf unconvincingly.

The Boff, who was keeping watch by the window, suddenly cried out. 'They're climbing up the walls.'

They all rushed to the window and looked down. Sure enough, the vampires had started to climb up the walls. They could see the black wings sprouting out of their backs and their hands and legs were acting like suckers gripping the wall. Their faces had developed little snub noses and their eyes were jet black. Soon every wall was a heaving mass of crawling black creatures hissing and spitting as they climbed.

'We need garlic,' said the Boff. 'They hate garlic.'

'Hold on. Let me have a look,' said Pigboy

sarcastically. He patted and then rummaged through his pockets. 'Oh no. I seem to be right out of garlic.'

'In the freezer,' said Tich. 'We've got garlic bread in the freezer.' He rushed off downstairs jumping down the steps two, three at a time and opened the door to the living room.

'Did you know, Kevin, that you can get wallpaper that looks exactly like wood-panelling? We might get some of that.'

Tich ignored his mother, rushed into the kitchen and grabbed two bags of sliced garlic bread. In seconds he was across the living room and back up the stairs.

'What did he take?' asked his mother

'Looked like garlic bread to me,' said Darren

'What would they want with garlic bread for?' queried Tich's mum. 'It's frozen.'

'Maybe they eat it like a lolly,' suggested Darren

'Kids these days! I don't know what gets into them.'

Tich handed the garlic bread round and they all took stations by open windows. 'When I say *now*,' said Tich. 'One two three GO!'

The others hesitated. 'What's the matter?' asked Tich.

'You haven't said *now* yet.'

'I said "Go," didn't I? Alright. Now. GO.'

They began to bombard the vampire children with garlic bread. Several were almost at the bedroom windows. The leading vampires fell away in disgust at the stink of garlic.

'It's working,' said Thicko. The garlic bread seemed to act like acid on the vampires, giving off smoke as it burned into their skins. They fought to brush it off but the garlic bread was sticky. They twisted and turned in fear and pain, all the while making their unearthly screeching sounds.

'That's it. That's all we've got,' said Tich, once the garlic bread was exhausted.

The vampires were babbling in confusion in the garden. Some were tearing the garlic bread off their faces. The sticking garlic tore away their skin and left bloody patches of exposed flesh.

But gradually the rest of the vampires were overcoming their fear and calming themselves. Their bloodshot eyes turned upward towards their prey staring at them from the bedroom windows. Their eyes burned red with anger and they began, once again, to crawl up the walls.

'Haven't you got any more garlic?' demanded Pigboy.

'No,' said the Boff, turning out his pockets, 'I seem to have clean run out.' Pigboy glared at him. Even the Boff was talking back to him now. He'd have to put a stop to that, but fighting the vampires was the priority for the moment.

'No, that was the lot,' said Tich. 'Oh hold on. We might have some garlic mini-kievs.' Once again he bounded down the stairs and returned with a large pack of ASDA Mini Garlic Kievs.

'What was it this time?' asked Tich's mum.

'Looked like garlic mini-kievs,' replied Darren.

'What would they want with frozen garlic mini-kievs?'

'Perhaps they like to suck 'em like gobstoppers,' suggested Darren.

'It's just attention seeking, that's all it is,'

said Tich's mum. 'There's such a thing as stairs you know,' she shouted at the strange black creatures crawling up the outside walls of the house. 'I'm going to ignore them. It's the only way to deal with it. What's on next?'

Darren checked in his magazine. 'It's Patio People.'

'Ooh, lovely,' said Tich's mum as she popped another Malteser into her mouth

Chapter Sixteen

Curse of the Mummy

Tich handed round the mini-kievs and they began throwing them at the vampires which were crawling up the walls, encasing the house in a seething black mass.

The children found if you could get a direct hit on the head of a vampire it would knock them off the wall completely, often taking two or three other vampires with them. They tried to hold back until the last minute when the repulsive little faces appeared at the window sill and they were sure of a direct hit on their faces.

But the attack was relentless and the mini-kievs were running low. It was only a matter of moments before they ran out completely. For every vampire knocked down, two or three more would appear to attack the walls. They couldn't hold back the waves of ravenous, blood-thirsty creatures.

'There's too many of them,' said Maggs. 'We can't hold them off for much longer.'

'What are we going to do?'

'The *Imaginator*,' said the Boff. 'We've got to use the *Imaginator*.'

'What's he talking about?' asked Pigboy

Tich didn't answer. His father had given him the 'IDEAL'S IMAGINATOR' which allowed him to go anywhere in a fraction of a second. Tich had already travelled to meet Robin Hood and to fight a dragon. But there wasn't enough time to explain all that to Pigboy.

Tich pulled the mirror and the Guvnor out of the box. 'Right,' he said, 'everyone gather round me.' Tich would up the Guvnor. Dozens of black figures were now scrabbling at the windows, banging and screeching in a frenzy, their red saliva dribbling down the glass.

They were screaming out 'Blood, blood, give us your blood.' One of the windows shattered. Tich released the catch on the Guvnor just as the hoards poured in through the windows.

The Boff called out, 'What about the picture? You forgot the picture.'

'There's no time, no time,' called out Tich, his voice fading away into the distance.

The walls around them slowly started to move as if the whole house was turning around them. The walls moved faster and faster. The black figures, the windows and the house itself became just a blur of lines spinning around them and then the children felt as if they were ascending through the roof of the house and up into the sky. From above they could see Tich's house surrounded on all sides by a festering mass of evil.

On the bed in Tich's room was the *The Boys' Big Book of Vampires* lying open at the centre page. The picture was of a snow-covered forest with mountains in the distance; nestling half way up the mountain was an ancient gothic castle. In the foreground was a small inn and somewhere, far up above the mountains, was a black creature circling the peaks.

As they flew through the air Tich remembered that he should have brought Mum and Darren with them. They'd left them behind in Tich's house surrounded it five hundred blood crazed vampires.

Still. It was Tich's mum we are talking about here.

No contest really.

Chapter Seventeen

Pardon Me Boss, Is This The Transylvania Station?

The seven children had a soft landing in the thick white snow. For Tich's gang, their arrival was no great surprise, but for Pigboy, Thicko and Barf this was the first time abroad in time and space.

'What happened?' said a dazed Pigboy.

'This isn't Tich's bedroom. It's been snowing,' said Thicko observantly.

'Where are we?' asked Barf, entirely bemused. 'Is this a dream or what?'

Pigboy cuffed him around the head

'Does that feel like a dream?'

'No.'

'Then it's not a feppin dream is it, you tonk?'

'Why do you have to hit him?' asked Tich.

'I can hit who I like,' replied Pigboy.

'He's supposed to be your mate,' said Maggs. 'And anyway, you can't hit me because if you do I'll stick this fist right down your throat, you fat tucker.'

Pigboy was taken aback. He wasn't used to being talked to like that. He ought to punish her, but he was wary. Maggs wasn't like any other girl he'd ever come across. He let it pass.

'You're not in a dream,' said the Boff patiently. 'We have this way of travelling through time and space.'

'Like Doctor Who?' asked Barf.

'Yeah, like Doctor Who only we don't have a Tardis. We have the Guv …'

'Ssshh,' said Tich. 'We have these pictures and we know how to get into them.'

'So what picture are we in?'

Tich looked blank. He'd forgotten about the picture. 'Ah well, because we were in a hurry we didn't actually have time to chose one. We were surrounded by vampires, remember.'

'If there wasn't a picture, how do we know where we are?' asked Barf.

'My guess,' speculated the Boff. 'Is that we're in Transylvania.'

'Transylvania? Why?' asked Pigboy.

'Tich had this book on his bed, remember. *The Boys' Big Book of Vampires*. It was open in the centre pages. There was a picture of Transylvania. Which is where Dracula comes from. And I reckon that castle up there on the hill,' – they all looked up – 'that belongs to Dracula.'

A lone wolf cried plaintively from the forest on the mountainside. All the children shivered. They weren't dressed for the winter. They were surrounded by snowdrifts and the sun was getting low in the sky.

'I think we should go to that inn over there,' said Tich. 'We need somewhere to get out of the cold.'

They walked over to the old inn nestling in the trees at the edge of a clearing. The sign was swinging and creaking in the wind. The children peered through the windows but they were dirty and they couldn't see much in the gloom – just a few murky shadows moving about.

They tried the door but it was locked. The Boff banged loudly with the ancient metal door-knocker. 'Clunk, clunk, clunk.' Nothing happened.

Pigboy barged the Boff out of the way and banged the door-knocker as hard as he could. 'CLUNK, CLUNK, CLUNK.' The noise was deafening. After a few minutes, the door creaked open just enough for a single eye to peer through and inspect the shivering children.

'Yes?' said a voice suspiciously.

'Let us in, it's cold out here.'

'You can't come in,' said the voice in a strange Cornish accent.

'Why not? You're meant to be an Inn. You're supposed to welcome people.'

'Not round here, me dear. You be strangers. Strangers from far away, I'll be bound. Up to no good I imagine. There's no inns round here.'

'But there's a big sign hanging up there,' said Pigboy. 'It says "The Inn, All Welcome".'

'Oh, that sign. I see what you mean. Yes, that could be a sign for an inn, I can see you might think that, but it ain't.'

'What is it then?'

'I be paintin' it for a friend o' mine. It's just hanging up there to dry.'

Maggs was looking though the gap. 'But I can see tables and a bar and a fire.'

'I'm just looking after them for a friend.'

'Why are you lying to us?'

'We don't like strangers roun' here. Not no way, no.'

'So who are all those people drinking in the bar.'

'Oh them people! I didn't notice 'em. They be my cousins. They'll all be going 'ome soon.'

'Look. It's getting dark and we don't have anywhere to shelter. You've got to let us in,' said Tich.

A lone wolf howled from the forest.

'Hear that? That's a wolf. It's not safe out here.'

'No, no. That be no wolf. That be me dog, Rover. He'd be probably burying a bone or something, the rascal.'

Other wolves took up the cry and the valley seemed to be filled with mournful wailing.

'See. He's with his friends. They're all at it now. They get all playful in the evenings. Just tickle 'em under the chin. They love it.'

'They're not dogs. They're wolves and they're coming for us. You've got to let us in,' said Maggs.

'We're full up.'

'It says "Vacancies" in the window.'

'It was meant to say "No Vacancies" but I don't know how to spell "No". We're expectin' a last minute rush, see. Always happens on a Friday. All the rooms be taken. You'll be fine. There's no danger roun' here. Very few people go missin'. Anyway I've got to go now. You have a lovely day, mind.'

The door slammed shut and the children looked at each other

'What do we do now?' asked Thicko. 'It's getting cold, and dark and them wolves are getting nearer.'

'The only way back is through the mirror,' said Tich and, if we go through there, we'll just be where we started – surrounded by vampires.'

The sun was only just above the horizon now, the snow was falling in flurries and the wolves were wailing their eerie lament.

Tich peered out into the darkness. 'There's something coming.'

Chapter Eighteen

Stage Fright

They listened carefully and, after a minute, they could all hear the sound of approaching horses. A black carriage led by four horses came into sight and thundered towards them. It was being driven by a figure whose face was hidden by a black hood. The children stood to one side as it seemed to be going straight past them but, at the last minute, the hooded figure pulled on the reins and brought the carriage to a halt directly in front of the children.

The driver said nothing and did not even look down. The horses' breath sent out clouds of white vapour and steam was rising from their flanks as they whinnied and pawed the ground. The hooded figure still did not move, just stared straight ahead, its face hidden.

After a moment the door to the carriage

swung open and the children peered inside. No one came out.

'I think we're supposed to get in it,' said Pigboy.

'I don't like the look of it,' said the Boff. 'Where are you going?'

There was no reply.

'It looks nice and warm in there,' said Ginger.

'I don't like it,' said the Boff.

'What else are we going to do?' said Maggs. 'Stay here and freeze to death?'

Maggs stepped forward and peered into the carriage. The upholstery was a fiery red colour and all the seats were empty. She slowly and gingerly stepped inside. 'Come on. We don't have any choice, do we?'

The others climbed aboard and sat down on the comfortable plush seats. The door swung closed and there was a clunk as it locked. The hooded figure cracked the whip and seconds later they were racing recklessly along the bumpy road, the forest a blur through the windows.

When the carriage went around a corner, two wheels lifted off the ground, throwing the children from one side to the other. After a mile or so the road forked and the carriage turned to the right and began to ascend a mountain road. The carriage continued up at the same pace.

'This is like that ride on Alton Towers,' said Barf. 'I think I might throw up.'

'Yeah, that was on the Teacup Ride. You threw up all over that Brownie 'cause you're nothing but a big girl,' said Pigboy.

'I did not.'

'Did.'

'Did not.'

'Did.'

'Will you two shut up please. I'm trying to think,' said the Boff.

'I wondered what all that clanking was,' said Pigboy.

'It's a bit steep,' said Ginger peering out of the window. The road had now started to climb the side of the mountain with a steep cliff rising up one side and a sheer drop at the other. The road was only just wide enough to fit along the ledge but the driver did not reduce the speed as the carriage bounced and skidded often perilously close to the yawning chasm to the left.

'Look at that,' said Maggs

They looked up out of the window and there above them was the dark grey castle they had seen in the distance. It was built into the side of the cliff with sheer drops on three sides. They could see the road leading along beside the cliff and then across a bridge before disappearing into the castle itself.

The carriage took a bend suddenly and two wheels to the right lifted clear off the ground giving the children a sickening view of the drop below. Rocks lying on the road were being knocked off the cliff edge.

Barf, Thicko and Ginger had closed their eyes and stuck their fingers in their ears. Any moment now, the coachman was going to make an error and they'd career off the road and plunge into the ravine below to certain death. It only seemed a matter of time.

They all felt great relief when, a little further on, the carriage began to slow as it approached the stone bridge. The bridge had crumbled away at the edges and the low stone walls on either side had wide gaps. The wheels of the carriage only just fitted in the gap between the walls. Half way across the carriage stopped completely.

'What's he stopped here for?' asked Tich.

He looked out of the window and could see, just ahead, the reason – a large chunk of the bridge to the right had fallen away completely, leaving a gap where the wheels could easily become wedged.

The carriage began to edge forward slowly. They felt a jerk as the front wheel dropped into the gap and then pulled up the other side. A second later the coach jerked again as the rear wheel dropped down into the gap, but this time the carriage stopped, the wheel wedged in place.

Small stones bounced off the wheels and disappeared into the darkness. The coachman whipped the horses and the coach jerked forward, but without enough impetus to pull free. A large rock gave way and the carriage lurched to the right.

'Are we safe yet?' asked Ginger, opening his eyes and taking his fingers out of his ears.

'No,' said Maggs

Ginger put his fingers back in his ears, shut his eyes and began to hum to himself.

The coachman lashed the horses again and they whinnied in protest. The right wheel edged upwards against the sheer stone, finally getting a grip on the rough surface. It was almost at the top when this stone itself fell away. Just in time the rear wheel rolled clear of the gap and brought the carriage forward off the bridge and on to solid ground.

As they did so, more large stones were dislodged and, for a second, it seemed as if the whole bridge was going to collapse, but a few rocks in the middle held firm. All that remained was a single arc of stones less then half a metre wide. It was obvious that the carriage would never cross the bridge again and was trapped forever in the dark castle.

Chapter Nineteen

Out for the Count

The carriage had pulled into a courtyard. The driver climbed down, secured the brakes and disappeared off into one of the doorways. The carriage door swung open.

'How does it do that?' queried the Boff inspecting the door to see if there was a mechanism to make it open and close automatically. He moved it backwards and forwards but could see nothing.

'It's a magic door,' said Ginger

'Nothing's magic,' said the Boff dismissively.

Maggs walked round trying the doors in the courtyard. All were locked except one. She pulled the door open. 'Come on,' she shouted at the others. 'It's freezing out here.' They all followed except the Boff who was still experimenting with the carriage door.

Tich came back and dragged him away.

They found themselves in a large open hall. On the far side was a roaring fire which the children gathered round warming their freezing hands. Above them was a high vaulted ceiling and the four walls were hung with huge dusty tapestries depicting murderous battles. The hall was lit with gas lamps that lined the walls.

In the middle was a heavy oak table surrounded with seven chairs. On the table were hams, chickens, bread, fruit, biscuits, in fact virtually anything and everything you could possibly eat. Barf stepped forward to try a biscuit. Thicko knocked it out of his hand. 'Don't eat that,' he said. 'It might be poisoned.'

'Poisoned!' exclaimed Pigboy. 'They could have killed us about a million times already – they could have just left us out in the cold, set the wolves on us, or chucked us over a cliff, or dropped us off that bridge. They didn't bring us all this way to poison us. That's the most stupid thing you've ever said. And that's saying something for an ignoramicus like you,' and with that he broke a leg off a chicken and bit out a huge chunk which he proceeded to chew vigorously.

Suddenly he grasped his stomach and lurched forward. 'Oh no. Oh no. You were right. It *is* poisoned.' He fell to the ground groaning, clutching his stomach and wailing. Then he stopped, laughed out loud, jumped up and said, 'Well, if it's all poisoned, I'd better keep it for myself.'

The others needed no further invitation to start grabbing the food from the table. They realised they'd had nothing to eat since breakfast time and were starving.

No one said a word as they steadily devoured their way though virtually everything until the top of the table looked as if someone had tossed in a grenade. After half an hour they were lounging on the chairs holding their stomachs.

At the far end of the hall were two flights of stone steps leading to an ancient oak door. There was a loud creak as the door swung open and they all looked up. A figure in a long grey coat swept out onto the landing, his head hidden by a black hood.

'Good evening,' he said and as the children all turned to face him, he pulled the hood back to reveal a pasty-white face, rheumy red eyes and lank grey hair.

'It's Draclea,' said Ginger.

'Dracula. It's Dracula. *Count* Dracula, if you don't mind.'

'Told you it was Draclea,' whispered Ginger.

'Welcome to my castle. I see by the remains on the table you have eaten well.'

'It wasn't us. It was them other big boys,' said Barf.

'Don't worry. The food was there for you to enjoy. It was intended for you. You are my honoured guests. I want you to feel at home. We Transylvanians are famous for our hospitality.'

'Try telling that innkeeper,' murmured Tich.

'Ah yes, the locals. They are full of superstition, you know. They believe the most outrageous things. They think Ghoulies and Ghosties are abroad at night. They shut their doors at dusk and don't open them till the sun is high in the sky. They are primitive fools. They even believe in vampires. But vampires don't exist, isn't that true, Pravin?'

'How does he know my name?' asked the Boff.

'I know all your names and all about you. I do not invite just anyone to my castle you know. I like only the civilised and sophisticated ...'

Barf belched loudly. 'Sorry about that,' he said.

'And the witty,' continued the Count. 'Now I'm afraid I have urgent business to attend. You will find your rooms fully prepared and at the far end of the hall. I must ask you to confine yourself to this wing of the castle. You will have noticed the castle is not as it was. The other areas of the castle are far too dangerous for children. We have lost many rooms to the chasm. The safety of my guests is important to me,' and with that he pulled his hood over his face and swept back out of the door. There was a loud clank as he locked the door behind him.

'Right,' said Pigboy. 'I say we get out of here right now.'

'It's dark out there,' said Thicko.

'Maybe, but if we stop here, he'll come after us. That's why he's brought us. He wants to suck all our blood and then we'll all die and come back as vampires,' said Pigboy.

'He's right,' said Tich, not believing he'd ever agree with anything Pigboy had said. He was beginning to realise that there are worse things in the world than Pigboy.

'We can't go across that bridge in the dark,' said Tich. 'It's too dangerous. And you know what that path down is like, and then there's the forest and the wolves and he'll be looking for us. He'll turn into a bat and be able to see in the dark. We can't get out of here now. We need to wait till daylight. He won't be able to fly in the day. All we've got to do is get through the night here.'

The others nodded in agreement. The door at the far end of the hall was open and it led into a corridor off which was a series of very similar rooms each with its own small fireplace, bed and washstand. There were many rooms but only seven had made up beds and fires burning, with candles lit by the bedside.

It was late now and the children were feeling exhausted. The beds looked warm and comfortable, with thick white sheets and their covers made from eiderdown.

Maggs said, 'I've had it. I'm going to go to bed.'

'But what if Draclea comes in the night?' asked Ginger.

'If he comes near me,' said Maggs, 'I'll rip his feppin head off.'

The boys nodded their heads in appreciation. Maggs *v* Dracula. It could go either way.

Chapter Twenty
Flying Tonight

Maggs was woken in the night by a scrabbling noise at her window. She couldn't see anything in the darkness outside but there appeared to be something trying to get into her room. The candle was burning low and the fire in the grate was nearly out.

She pulled the bedcovers up. The noise continued and somehow the thing on the outside managed to open the window. Maggs could just make out what appeared to be a giant bat trying to squeeze through the window. A few more moments and she could see that was exactly what it was and it was almost through.

Seconds later, it had forced itself into the room and it flapped its wings a little and then settled on the floor. Its face was like a cross between a pig and a mouse and it had huge pointed ears. Its mouth was open with two long blood-stained incisors at the top. It was making a strange squeaking sound.

It opened its wings and flapped them. Then it retracted them and they disappeared behind a black cape. The features of the bat blurred and were transformed into human form. The hairy face turned chalk white, and blood red lips and cold black eyes were revealed. The blood stained incisors did not change and Maggs recognised the malevolent outline of Count Dracula.

He had a strange grimace on his face as he circled his prey, saying nothing but with saliva pouring out of his mouth. He approached the bed, towering over the tiny form that was Maggs huddled in the bedclothes. He leant forward slowly and Maggs could smell his foul putrid breath on her face.

As his face came towards her, he turned his head and his mouth opened wide as it prepared to bite into her neck.

Suddenly Maggs produced a kitchen folk and rammed it hard into Dracula's neck. Dracula staggered backwards with blood pouring from his wounded neck as she threw off the bedclothes. He was making unearthly squealing noises as he fell back in agony.

'Now!' a voice shouted and six small figures emerged from under the bed. Each was armed with a stick or a chair leg or whatever had come to hand and they set about Dracula, beating him, poking him, smacking him, tripping him, anything to beat him back.

At first the Count fell back in surprise, but then he began to retaliate. He grabbed Tich's leg, swung him round and threw him against the wall. He lashed out, hitting Ginger across the head. He grabbed Pigboy's arm and twisted it. Dracula was as strong as twelve men and lethally dangerous as he struck out in fear and anger.

But just as it seemed that the Vampire was going to overwhelm and kill them all, he stopped fighting, stepped back and stood still for a second. He looked towards the window where the first rays of morning were beginning to pierce the darkness. He moved back towards the window and opened it wide.

Turning, he faced the children one last time

and hissed, 'Enjoy your last day on earth. By tomorrow night you'll all join me and we shall feast on blood together.' He cackled with laughter and climbed through the window and launched himself into the air.

The children rushed to the window and looked down into the chasm below. At first it looked as though the Count would fall to his death, smashed on the rocks below. But, as he tumbled down the cliff, his body began to transform. Long dark wings extended out of his back and he swooped above the rocks and away from the cliff. Then in a low wide arc he circled back round towards the castle.

Chapter Twenty-One

A Bridge Too Far

The sky was lightening and the dawn was coming. Far below, the bat flapped its wings and landed on the rocks at the base of the castle. It looked up and the children instinctively drew back from the window. When they looked again it was crawling away out of sight into its lair somewhere in the bowels of the castle.

The children breathed a sigh of relief, but they knew that their ordeal was far from over. If they were to survive, they needed to get away from this terrible place and to do it before the sun set again.

They rested for a while and eventually fell asleep. By the time they woke up, the sun was high in the sky and when they went back into the hall, they were surprised to find the table laid out with a huge breakfast – eggs, bacon, toast, sausages – more than enough for a dozen people. They ate silently and hungrily, the fear in their hearts subsiding for the time being.

Once they'd finished eating, they discussed what to do. 'The only way out is across that bridge,' said the Boff.

'It's not safe. It's falling down,' said Ginger.

'There's no other way down, unless you fancy jumping,' said Tich.

They trooped down to the yard and were surprised to find that the main gates were not locked. They were big heavy oak doors which, being so well balanced, could be pushed open just by leaning on them.

The children inspected the condition of the bridge. It seemed reasonably solid at the edges where the buttresses that supported it still looked fully intact, but, in the middle, where the side walls had fallen away completely, all that was left was a single narrow arc of crumbling stone. They would have to walk across that span, with no walls on either side to protect them, and hope that it would bear their weight.

'We need a rope,' said Tich.

'I think I saw one in one of the bedrooms,' said the Boff and he set off in search of it.

'So who's going to try and walk across it?' asked Pigboy.

All the boys looked down at the ground, while Maggs, predictably, stepped forward and said, 'I'll go.'

'Not this time,' said Tich. 'You always take all the risks. Someone else should do it for a change.' He looked around at the others. They all averted their eyes and no one said anything.

'Looks like it's going to be me then,' said Tich. He stepped up to the bridge and looked down into the chasm and felt his confidence drain away like water on a sandy beach. When he swallowed, he felt a large lump in his throat and just for one second he was tempted to step back and let Maggs take the lead again. But he knew it wasn't her job this time. He'd stepped up for it and he was going to have to live, or die, with his decision.

The Boff returned with a good thick length of rope. 'Tie this around your waist,' he said to Pigboy, who was taken aback to hear someone like the Boff giving him orders and, more surprisingly, did exactly what he was told.

Then the Boff brought the other end of the rope forward and tied it around Tich's waist. 'Are you sure you know how to do knots?' Tich asked the Boff.

'I used to be in the Scouts,' he replied. Tich nodded his head. Maybe if he'd known he was going to be dangled over a precipice, he'd have joined them and learned how to do useful things like knots. He wondered if the Scouts maybe had a 'Kill a Vampire' badge.

The Boff was giving out more orders. 'Now everybody get a grip on the rope and whatever you do, don't let go.' For some reason the Boff had taken control of the situation, maybe because crossing ravines was a Scouty sort of thing to do.

'OK?' said Tich

'OK,' said the Boff.

Tich took a step forward and then stepped out onto the bridge. It felt firm enough. Maybe it had only fallen away because the carriage was so heavy. Maybe it would more easily take the weight of one small boy. Maybe.

Tich moved forward carefully until he reached the centre of the bridge. He was breathing deeply and took a single step forward out onto the narrow section. He didn't want to look down, but he needed to make sure the stonework was solid underneath his feet. He was shaking so much he thought his legs might give way.

He took another step. Now he was too far forward to jump back. He could only keep moving forward.

One more step and he'd be in the centre of the bridge. Maybe it would have been better if he had crawled across the damaged section. It would have been less dignified but it would have felt an awful lot safer.

Another two steps and he was past halfway. Two more and he'd be safe on the solid part of the bridge on the other side. He just had to keep his nerve. He was shaking so badly now he thought the vibrations might actually dislodge the stones under his feet. The loose mortar between the stones was being blown about by the wind.

The stone under his back foot seemed to

twist a little. Maybe it was just his imagination. Then there was a jerk as the central section of the bridge dropped a fraction of a centimetre. In another second he was sure the entire section would fall away.

He did the only thing he could – he threw himself forward and grabbed for the solid stones on the other side, but, as he did so, the central part of the bridge gave way completely and the huge stones plummeted into the chasm. Tich grasped at the stones on the far side but they were smooth after centuries of wear and his hands could find no grip. Then he too fell through the gap. Only the rope could save him now.

The others had been concentrating so much on watching Tich that they had let their hold on the rope loosen. When the rope suddenly went taught, it slipped through their fingers and burned into their hands. Pigboy was yanked off his feet and crashed into them sending them all hurtling towards the wide gap where the bridge once had been.

The Boff, at the front, managed to keep a grip on the rope, dug in his heels and ploughed a deep furrow through the dirt until he skidded across the bridge and he too disappeared over the edge.

The other children, having finally realised what was happening, gripped the rope, dug their heels in, and pulled as hard as they could, dragging the Boff back to safety. But just as he had been hauled back over the edge, the rope went slack and they all fell over backwards.

The far end of the rope flew up into the air. There was no sign of Tich anywhere.

Chapter Twenty-Two

Vantastic

'Hello. Hello.'

A voice was calling from the other side of the bridge. The children stood up and brushed off the dust. 'You'll be the children from the Inn. I assumed you'd end up here. Is everyone safe?'

The children stared at the rather eccentrically dressed man who'd arrived on the far side of the bridge. He was wearing a deerstalker hat, a tartan three-piece suit and huge hobnail boots and he carried a large bag that looked like it was made of carpet.

'We've lost Tich. He fell down when the bridge collapsed.'

'That'd be the young feller down there would it?' He pointed down to the cliff below the bridge.

The children approached the edge and

looked down. Twenty metres down on a small ledge sat Tich waving up at them. 'Well stop feppin staring at me and chuck that rope down,' shouted Tich impatiently.

'In good time young fellow,' said the man on the far side. 'Stand by'

The man began to spin round and round, swirling his carpet bag until he'd built up enough impetus to let it go and send it flying across the gap. Ginger stepped up to catch it but the sheer force of the bag knocked him backwards and the bag landed on top of him.

'Well caught, that man,' said the stranger. 'Now stand back please.' He took a few steps backwards and then ran towards the bridge, gathering more and more speed, until he launched himself into the air, flew across the gap and landed in a pile of dust in front of the astonished children.

'Morning,' he said standing up and dusting himself down. 'Van Helsing's the name. General handyman – sinks cleared, drains unblocked, vampires defenestrated.'

'What's "defensiated"?' asked Ginger

'Thrown out of the window, dear boy. Any

chance you might you be suffering problems with vampires by any chance?'

'There's Draclea,' said Ginger.

'*Draclea* you say. Fiendish! Using a false name to put us off the scent. Is there no end to this man's cunning? You've seen him, I trust.'

'He's in the castle, somewhere,' said Maggs.

'Yes, and back to his old tricks,' he continued. 'I had heard. Thought I'd better come and see what's happening. Once Dracula's flapping about the place, all hell breaks loose. Quite literally. That's why they sent for me.'

'You're not scared of him, then? Not like those others at the Inn?'

'Turned you away, I hear. Don't like strangers round here, the locals, not when Dracula's on the prowl. Don't like strangers. Don't like locals. Don't like anyone in fact. But that's Transylvanians for you. Just don't let them breathe on you – you'll die of garlic poisoning.'

'Is somebody going to help me or are you going to chat all feppin morning,' called a plaintive voice from the cliff face.

'Good point,' said Van Helsing. 'Let's get your young fellow off that cliff and safe. He looks as though he might be a bit happier up here with us.'

Once they'd recovered a very irritated Tich from the cliff face, the children did their best to explain how they'd ended up at Castle Dracula.

'Tell me about this *Imaginator* again.'

'It's this game that let's you travel to anywhere that's in a picture,' explained the Boff.

'And these pictures, are they real? If the pictures were in a storybook, an imaginary place, could you go there too?'

The children pondered this for a while. The truth was that they didn't really know the answer. Tich had travelled to a land where there were dragons – was that a real world or one that only existed in the imagination of the person who'd drawn the picture?

'May I see the Guvnor?'

Tich was reluctant to hand over the Guvnor to anyone else. Without the Guvnor they could never go home, but he did so anyway.

Van Helsing inspected the Guvnor carefully – trying to see inside the inner workings.

'Hmm. Fascinating. What one could do with a tool like this? Anyway,' he said changing the subject and slipping the Guvnor into his pocket. 'This Dracula – what are we going to do about him?'

'Er ... the Guvnor?' said Tich

'Pardon?'

'The Guvnor. You put it in your pocket.'

'Did I? Did I indeed? There I go – absent minded as ever.' He retrieved the Guvnor from his pocket and handed it back to Tich. 'Now you already know my name is Van Helsing. Call me Abraham if you wish. Now perhaps you'll tell me who is who amongst such an illustrious band.'

The children introduced themselves and Van Helsing listened intently. When they had finished he asked them. 'What do you know about vampires?'

'They drink blood and they live forever,' said Thicko.

'They don't like garlic,' said Barf

'They don't have a reflection,' said Maggs

'What about you?' said Van Helsing, addressing the Boff. 'What about you? What do you know about vampires?'

'That they don't exist,' said the Boff

'Good boy. You stick to your guns. We're not all sheep are we? But for the moment, for the sake of argument, you will have to accept that where we are right now, you need to be ready to fight vampires, whether they really exist or not. Do you agree with me?'

'Yes,' said the Boff smiling – and smiling was something the Boff rarely did, because there were always too many difficult things to think about.

'I'll tell you some things about vampires shall I – or more specifically how you fight them and how you kill the blighters. They don't have reflections as you say, but neither do they have shadows. At night they can turn into bats and fly, or wolves and hunt. They have the strength of ten men. They don't like garlic and they don't like the crucifix. Which is why you'll need these.' He handed out small silver crucifixes to hang around their necks and then he gave them garlands of dried garlic. 'Stuff this in your pockets and your collar.'

'They live forever which is a bit of a problem for me because I don't. But if you can put a stake through their hearts, cut off their heads and stick garlic down their necks it can keep them out of mischief for a few hundred years at least.' He paused. 'What time is it?'

'Nearly midday.'

'Right. That means we've got about four hours before the sun disappears behind those mountains. After that we're in trouble. Do you know where he goes in the day?'

'There's a window right at the bottom of the castle. Down there.' Pigboy pointed to the spot on the sheer cliff face where they'd seen Dracula enter the castle.

'Mmm, pity. We can't climb down there. We'll just have to go through the castle. And we'll need some weapons.' Van Helsing opened the carpet bag and removed a thick belt which he tied around his waist. He then attached a series of weapons and implements to the belt – wooden stakes, knifes, saws, mallets and so on.

They went back into the courtyard. 'All the doors are locked,' explained Maggs. 'You can only get to the hall and the bedrooms from the courtyard.'

'If anything should happen to me,' said Van Helsing, 'use these things in my belt to destroy any vampires we find. You must plunge one of these stakes directly into each of their hearts. Then you must saw off their heads ...'

'I'll do that,' said Maggs. 'I'm good at that.'

'Ughhh, gross,' said Thicko.

'Saw off their heads,' continued Van Helsing, 'and stuff garlic down their necks. That means the head cannot re-attach itself. Only then will you all be safe.' He paused.

'Remember, if we fail, then we'll all spend the rest of eternity sleeping in a coffin in the day and seeking blood every night. And let me tell you – there are much better ways of spending eternity.'

Chapter Twenty-Three

Down Down Deeper and Down

Van Helsing moved around the courtyard examining each door carefully. Finally he stopped at a large hand-carved old oak door. The carvings were of faces, all of them ugly and distorted. 'This is the one,' said Van Helsing.

'How do you know?' asked the Boff.

'Look at the spider's webs round the edge of the door. This is the only one where they're broken. And look at these fresh scratches around the lock. There's been a key in this one recently.' Pigboy rattled the door but it was firmly locked.

'Anybody know how to pick a lock?' asked Van Helsing

The children shook their heads.

'Not even you, George?' asked Van Helsing.

Pigboy shook his head. Tich was taken aback by how much Van Helsing seemed to know about them.

'Well, we're a bit short of time, aren't we? Probably need to get on,' said Van Helsing. 'Perhaps you'll all oblige me by retiring to a safe distance.'

The children stared at him. 'I think he means *get out of the way*,' explained the Boff, as Van Helsing produced a stick of dynamite from his belt, wedged it in the lock and lit the fuse with a match.

The children all ran for cover. Van Helsing strolled behind them and joined them behind a stone stairway. 'Right ... about ... now ... ' he said.

The fuse burned down and for a second seemed to have sputtered out, but after a moment's pause, there was a loud crack and a burst of smoke and, where the lock had been, there was now a gaping hole surrounded by shattered wood. Van Helsing approached the door, which swung open obligingly. He turned back to the children. 'Coming?' he asked and they all trooped after him.

Chapter Twenty-Four

Stairway to Hell

Van Helsing led the children confidently through the maze of dark corridors, flanked by ancient oak doors with carvings of beheadings and murder. Van Helsing stopped at one door and invited the children to take a look inside. The door opened on to a huge banqueting hall, lit by thick shafts of light coming from windows at the very tops of the walls.

They approached a table on which, though festooned with spider's webs and thick with dust, they could still make out the remains of a meal. There was every imaginable type of food laid out from whole pigs to swans, and pies the size of pillows – all half eaten and grey with age. Ginger picked up what looked like an apple and it crumbled to dust in his hands.

Maggs pointed at the pig's head and said

to Pigboy, 'That's your cousin, that is.' Pigboy chose to ignore her

'They don't eat,' explained Van Helsing. 'At least, not any more. All they crave is blood. Just think of it – all eternity and not even a slab of chocolate or a toffee apple.'

'What, not even a McDonald's Happy Meal,' queried Barf in horror.

'Not even that, whatever a McDonald's Happy Meal may be. A life without food is hardly worth living. It's our job to stop these people and put an end to all this evil and, do you realise, right now, we're the only people in the world who can do it. Come on.'

After what seemed an endless array of corridors and stairs, they finally reached the far corner of the castle, in a tower directly above the window into which Dracula had disappeared. They reached a door set into a circular wall.

'No cobwebs,' said Tich. 'And no scratches round the door.'

'Good boy,' said Van Helsing. 'You're learning.'

'Dynamite?' suggested Pigboy.

'I don't think so,' Van Helsing replied. We don't want to wake the dead before we're ready for them. Tich, can I borrow the Guvnor for a moment?'

Tich looked doubtful. 'You'll get it back, I promise.' Tich reluctantly handed over the Guvnor. Van Helsing gave it a quarter turn, held it against the lock and released the catch. There was a whirring sound as the cogs and wheels turned. From within the lock came the sound of metal grating against metal and then a loud clunk. Van Helsing tried the door and it opened.

'How did you know it was going to do that?' asked the Boff.

'What you have there,' said Van Helsing, handing it back to Tich, 'is one of the most sophisticated tools in the entire universe. Look after it. It might be the only one, ever.'

They followed Van Helsing through the door. There was a small balcony jutting out into the vast empty space that was the North Tower. It was a huge circular shaft with no floors, running from the battlements to the foundations below.

It was so far down you couldn't actually see the bottom. The top was open to the skies so the inside was lit with a bright glaring light from above. Because it was open, the walls were damp and covered in algae and there was the constant sound of dripping water.

As their eyes grew accustomed to the light, they noticed, running from the top to the bottom of the shaft, a curved stairway that clung to the walls of the tower. It was just wide enough for one person to climb at a time. It was old and crumbled and green with slime.

The children realised with horror that this was to be their way down – one long slippery, decrepit stone stairway with no handrail. There were some handholds cut into the walls but these were no doubt hosts to spiders and centipedes and a myriad of creepy-crawlies.

'Who has a head for heights?' asked Van Helsing.

There was a long silence.

'I don't think I can do it,' said the Boff.

'Good boy. That's honest.'

'I'll go,' said Maggs.

'I knew you'd be the first,' said Van Helsing.

'OK,' said Pigboy.

'I'm in,' said Tich.

There was no reply from Thicko, Barf and Ginger. They stood, knees quaking, flattened against the wall at the back of the balcony.

'You lads stay here and stand guard,' said Van Helsing, winking at Tich. 'We all have our fears to overcome, don't we? You've shown willing, that's the important thing. You four stay here. If we're not back when the light starts to fade go back to your rooms and wait there.'

'But what if you don't come back at all?' asked Ginger.

'Then we are all in deep trouble, my friend, deep, deep trouble.' He paused. 'Right, follow me the three of you.' He started off down the staircase and Tich, Maggs and Pigboy came after.

The steps were worn and slippery and their progress was slow at first. Van Helsing would stop occasionally and warn them of a particularly dangerous step. Van Helsing never lost his foothold once but the children did, constantly bumping into the person in front.

Sometimes all three of them would lose their balance and end up crushed against Van Helsing but he was strong and solid and stopped them falling.

The further down they stepped the darker it became. As Pigboy approached a step that was nearly worn away completely, he put his hand in a crevice to steady himself and then squealed loudly as something stung his hand. He pulled his hand out of the crevice to reveal a half-metre long centipede clinging on to his fingers.

He shook his hand violently but the centipede hung on for grim death, refusing to budge. Pigboy slammed it against the wall until it finally let go and disappeared into the abyss below.

'Are you all right?' asked Van Helsing.

'Yeah,' said Pigboy, cradling his hand which was already starting to throb.

They continued on in the darkness, only able to see the steps from the grey light reflecting off the damp surface.

Pigboy was getting left behind. His hand was hurting too much for him to steady himself against the wall. So when he slipped on a particularly greasy step, he couldn't stop himself falling forward into Maggs who also lost her footing and bumped into Tich.

Tich turned round to see that Pigboy was about to fall and grabbed his leg and braced himself. He found himself hanging onto Pigboy's leg as he dangled dangerously in thin air. For a moment Tich remembered how he'd dreamed of doing this to Pigboy in revenge for all the humiliation and pain that he'd inflicted on Tich over the years. In other circumstances he might have just let him go.

But right now the real enemy was Dracula and Pigboy was on his side. Van Helsing grabbed another leg and Maggs helped Tich drag Pigboy back to safety. They all sat down on the steps to catch their breath and to recover their nerve.

They seemed to have been descending for hours and there still was no sign of the floor at the bottom of the tower.

'Come on,' said Van Helsing, and moments later they resumed their downward journey, albeit with nerves jangling and a sense of foreboding for what was to come.

Chapter Twenty-Five
Stake and Flips

It took them nearly an hour to descend to the floor of the tower using up precious time before the sun would set and the fight against Dracula would resume on his terms in the dark.

When they finally reached it, they found the door at the bottom was not locked. Whoever was inside would not expect anyone to make it down the crumbling stairway.

The door creaked a little as they slowly pushed it open, not wishing to give notice to anyone that they'd arrived. Van Helsing produced a wooden torch from his belt and set it blazing. They followed the corridor around until Van Helsing stopped at a window.

'See the claw marks,' he said. 'This is the window that Dracula uses to access his lair. It won't be much further now.'

They opened another door and found a room that smelt dank and dirty. When they entered the room, they could see row upon row of wooden coffins.

'I thought it was just him,' said Pigboy.

'At the moment, yes,' said Van Helsing. 'But some of these coffins will be ours if we fail. What a place to spend eternity!' Pigboy shivered at the thought.

Van Helsing produced a crowbar from his belt and used it to open the lid of one of the coffins. Inside was a skeleton. It had a wooden stake through the ribs penetrating where the heart would have been. The skull was separate from the body and there were the remains of flowers stuffed into the top of the torso.

'Is that him?' asked Tich.

'No, sadly not,' said Van Helsing. 'This is one of his cohorts. When Dracula's ready he'll remove a stake and they will rise again. Some of these coffins will have skeletons, others will be empty. When we find Dracula you can be sure we will know him.'

Van Helsing closed the lid of the coffin. He produced more torches from his belt and lit them, handing them to the children. He ran his finger through the dust on the coffin lid. 'Find one that has no dust and we have our man,' he said.

The four of them split up and began inspecting the coffins. After a few moments, Maggs cried out. The others rushed over. She was standing over an elaborately carved wooden coffin with gold inlay and solid gold handles. Van Helsing ran his finger along the top. 'No dust. You're right. What's the time?'

Tich checked his watch. 'It's three thirty.'

'No time to lose, then.' Van Helsing jemmied open the lid and lifted it. Inside was the figure of Dracula quietly sleeping. His face was deathly white and his lips were stained with blood.

'Doesn't look a thousand years old, does he?' said Van Helsing. 'But he soon will.'

Van Helsing removed a stake, a jagged-edge knife and a mallet from his belt in preparation. He handed the jagged edged knife to Tich. 'Hold this ready,' he said.

He took the stake and placed it against where Dracula's heart would be. 'If you would be so kind as to hold this in place,' he asked Pigboy. 'If he wakes up, he's going to scream and wriggle so hold it firm. He doesn't want a stake through his heart any more than you would. Maggs, if he tries to sit up, hold him down till we have finished our work. There will be blood my friends. There will be blood.'

With the stake in place, Van Helsing stood back to take a long swing with his hammer. 'Ready?' he asked. Pigboy winced. If the hammer missed it would probably take his hand with it. Then with all his might, Van Helsing swung the hammer in a wide arc and brought it down with great precision on the stake and the stake plunged deep into the heart of Dracula.

There was silence. 'There's something wrong here,' said Van Helsing.

'You've killed him, haven't you?' asked Maggs.

'It's too easy. There's something wrong. Vampires don't just die. They fight for their lives.' Van Helsing inspected the coffin. 'We got the right one, didn't we?' He inspected the coffin lid. There was no dust and it'd been open recently. 'Unless ...'

'Unless what?' asked Tich.

'Unless this coffin was *made* to look like it was the one. In which case ...'

'In which case,' came a deep threatening voice from out of the darkness, 'Dracula is still alive.'

And with that Dracula launched himself across the room and knocked Van Helsing off his feet. Then he picked him up like a rag doll and threw him across the room. Van Helsing bounced off the wall and fell groaning to the floor.

Dracula grabbed Maggs and Pigboy and banged their heads together and tossed them away, bouncing across the coffins as they went.

He turned to face Tich who was cowering behind one of the coffins. 'I can see you. There's no hiding from me. You dare violate my crypt and disturb my followers. You have tried to kill Dracula and now you will pay the price. Now that coffin you hide behind will become your home for ever.'

Then he launched himself forward through

the air towards Tich. For a second Tich was frozen to the spot in fear. Dracula was flying through the air, his eyes burning red, his mouth of razor sharp teeth open and ready to tear out Tich's throat.

But just as the Vampire was about to descend on him, Tich remembered the knife Van Helsing had given him. He held it out in front of him. The Vampire did not have time to react and the knife plunged into his chest.

He landed heavily on Tich, enveloping him in his cloak and Tich found himself in complete darkness. The blood from the wound was pouring over him making him cough and splutter and gasp for breath as the weight of the creature bore down on him. Tich was drowning in blood.

Chapter Twenty-Six

Crumble and Fall

'What do we do if something happens to them?' asked Ginger. It had been nearly two hours and there was no sign of the others since they'd disappeared down the stairway into the darkness. The light in the tower was beginning to fade and the four children were growing anxious.

'If they don't come back, that means Dracula's got them. We'll have to go and hide somewhere until the morning,' said Thicko.

'But wherever we go, we're trapped,' said Barf. 'We can't get out of the castle. We can't get home. We're stuck here till he catches us.'

'If they don't come back, we'll just have to think about something else,' said the Boff firmly, although he didn't feel particularly firm inside. It was Tich who generally told him what to do. The Boff was immensely clever, but found the world a difficult place to deal with if Tich wasn't around.

He knew that Maggs would take the lead if she was here. But the Boff realised that, as things stood with Barf, Thicko and Ginger, it would be him who'd need to be in charge and, at the present time, he had no idea what they should do.

Suddenly there was a loud explosion and a flash from the bottom of the tower. The four children peered into the gloom to try to see what was happening. A great cloud of smoke billowed past them obscuring their vision. But even when it cleared they could still see nothing.

'Look, there,' said Thicko, pointing down to the far side of the tower. They could just make out signs of movement. Something or someone was coming up the stairway but they still could not make out who it was.

'It's Maggs,' said Ginger spotting the person leading the rush up the stairs. He could tell it was her from her scruffy hair, although she was too covered in dust from the explosion to make out much else.

Pigboy was next and then Tich and finally Van Helsing, who was falling behind. Maggs was soon at the balcony and they helped her up into safety. They did the same for the others until everyone was safe.

'What happened? You're covered in blood, Tich,' asked the Boff, immensely relieved at having the others back and someone apart from him to take charge.

'I was nearly crushed to death by that feppin vampire that's why. If Maggs and Pigboy hadn't dragged him off, I'd've drowned.'

'Who are you talking about?' asked Pigboy who had no idea that he had this nickname as no one had ever the nerve to use it to his face

'No time. No time,' said Van Helsing peered down into the gloom. 'He'll be here soon enough. Where's the bag?'

Van Helsing opened the bag and took out a dozen sticks of dynamite. 'We can't stake him now but we can slow him down a bit,' he said. He went back down the stairway and inserted the sticks of dynamite into crevices in the wall. 'I need your help, Tich.'

Tich climbed down the steps to join him.

'I haven't got time to light them all. You see the top six. Take these matches and light the fuses starting at the bottom. I'll light the others down here. Then we should have just enough time to get clear.'

Tich wasn't too happy about the word 'should'.

'He's coming. He's coming,' called out Maggs.

They looked down and there, circling upwards through the tower, were the giant black wings of the Vampire.

'Get clear you lot,' called up Van Helsing. 'Now Tich *go*.'

Tich climbed up the stairs and started lighting the sticks of dynamite. The matches were damp and hard to light so it was slow going, but finally he'd got the last one lit just when Van Helsing came up behind him and pushed him back onto the balcony.

The creature was circling closer and closer and as Van Helsing tried to push Tich through the door, it swooped down and grasped Tich in its claws and began to drag him back into the tower. Maggs grabbed a stake and started to rain blows on the Vampire's wings.

For a second it loosened its grip on Tich, and the children were able to drag him clear. A final blow across the face from Maggs forced the Vampire back and it fell away briefly before regaining its balance and preparing to launch a new attack.

Van Helsing pushed the children out of the door and along the corridor beyond.

Just as he did so, the first stick of dynamite exploded sending a ball of fire into the air and along the corridor towards the children. More sticks exploded, sending sharp fragments of rock out in all direction.

Some of these hit the Vampire, forcing it backwards. Another explosion knocked it to one side. Without its forward momentum, it stalled in the air and plummeted downwards. The remaining sticks of dynamite exploded and the entire wall came away, dragging the balcony with it.

The children and Van Helsing found themselves slipping down toward the gaping hole that had appeared in the side of the tower. They dragged themselves to safety along the corridor away from the tower.

With a large chunk of wall missing, the tower had become unstable and began to collapse inwards. Thousands of tons of stone began to crumble and fall. The tower was imploding and, for a moment, the children thought it would drag the entire castle with it, but it broke away from the rest of the stonework and, with a noise like a hundred thunderstorms all at once, the tower collapsed, burying the remains of the Vampire in a thousand-ton tomb.

A giant dust cloud enveloped the castle. Down at the Inn, the locals who had been watching in horror and amazement, crossed themselves over and over again.

'There goes the tourist trade,' said the innkeeper.

Chapter Twenty-Seven

Vampire Hunting for Dummies

The children and Van Helsing sat around the dining table eating what was left from their breakfast. They ate in silence too shocked and exhausted to speak. After they finished the food, they sat back and stared blankly, lost in their own thoughts.

After a while Van Helsing spoke. 'Well, now the job's done, I suppose we'd better get you all home.'

'We can't go home,' said Tich. 'We'll go straight back to the place we left – surrounded by vampires.'

'Tell me some more about these vampires of yours,' said Van Helsing and the children went over the story from the time they opened the mausoleum to the point where they were besieged in Tich's house.

'And there are too many to stake?'

'You can't go sticking stakes into people and cutting their heads off. Not where we come from. You're not allowed to do things like that,' explained the Boff

'How do you deal with vampires then?'

'We don't deal with them,' said Magg.

'Mainly because they don't exist,' added the Boff

'Ah well, that's difficult, but if they don't exist, where's your problem?' For the moment the Boff was lost for an answer.

Van Helsing was lost in his thoughts as he pondered the children's predicament. Finally he spoke. 'I don't think your problem is insoluble.'

Ginger stared blankly. 'I think I can help you,' he continued. 'With the right weapons, you can deal with these vampires.'

'We can't kill them,' said Barf. 'They'd send us to prison.'

'I think I have the weapon you need for the circumstances.'

'Is it like a nucula bomb?' asked Ginger.

'A *nuclear* bomb,' corrected the Boff.

'That what I said,' said Ginger, 'a nucula bomb to kill Draclea.'

The Boff groaned and hit his forehead with his hand.

'There is only one weapon the vampire fears,' interrupted Van Helsing. 'And that, my friends, is knowledge. I've killed thousands of vampires, not because I had more weapons, not because I was stronger, but because of this.' He pointed at his head. 'The human brain. They're just creatures, these vampires, strong and cunning perhaps, but in the end we will always defeat them. Because we have the intelligence.'

Ginger and Thicko nodded sagely in agreement.

Chapter Twenty-Eight

Garlic Dead

The hundreds of little vampires crowded into Tich's bedroom were bemused. The seven victims they had surrounded had somehow disappeared into thin air. One minute they were there, the next the bedroom was empty. The looked at each other perplexed, shrugged their shoulders and started to turn away.

But just as they were in the process of climbing back out of the windows, the seven children were back, all collapsed in a heap as if they'd fallen from a great height.

The vampires began to hiss and they resumed stalking their prey. The children formed into a tight circle, produced silver crucifixes from their pockets and held them high. The vampires cowered and grimaced, and stepped back. Gradually the children expanded their circle and forced the vampires out of the windows. When the last one had skulked away, the children held their crucifixes out of the window and drove the vampires back down the walls.

'What on earth are do you think you're doing?' Tich's mum thundered into the room. 'Darren and I are just trying to have a peaceful afternoon watching the television. Is that too much to ask? Apparently it is. We can't hear the television for all this banging and crashing and nonsense going on up here. Now we'll never know what the Wallpaper Hanging Top Five Tips were. And what are these?'

She grabbed Tich's cross and inspected it.

'That's a crucifix,' said Tich.

'What's it for?'

'For fighting vampires,' explained Ginger.

Tich's mum glared at him. 'I've told you that boy's a bit simple, Kevin. I don't why you insist on being friends with him. *Fighting vampires*. The nonsense you talk sometimes. There is no such thing as vampires.'

'Yes, there is,' said the Boff surprised to hear his own voice coming out with such a statement. 'Van Helsing gave them to us.'

'And who is this Van Helsing person?'

'He's this man who helped us.'

'Yes, and I heard about men like him. Now give me these crucifixes. All of you. And I don't want to hear about vampires ever again.'

One by one, the children reluctantly handed over their crucifixes.

'Why can't you play with normal toys Kevin, like frisbees. You never play with that Etch-a-Sketch I bought you in the car boot sale. Now if I hear any more noise, you're all going home. You see, I've already missed half of Wallpaper Surprise. Now just keep quiet, d'you hear?'

The children nodded in silence and Tich's mum went back down stairs.

The vampires on the outside walls were looking at each other, quizzically. They climbed back up to peer through the windows and when they realised there were no bright crucifixes to burn their eyes and fill them with terror, they resumed their attack.

The children huddled together in the centre of the room. Soon the vampires were back up on the window sill, saliva dribbling out of their mouths. They pushed the windows open and slithered down the walls. The ones behind pushing their way in, anxious not to miss out of the blood feast that was about to happen.

The children edged back towards the far wall and warily the vampires moved forwards. There were at least twenty vampires in the room now and more pouring in the window. There were no crucifixes. Nothing in their way. Any second now they would leap forward with fangs bared ready to tear out throats and feast on fresh blood.

'Now,' said Tich. The children removed the pins from the small round objects, they held in their hands and rolled them forward across the floor. The vampires scuttled away from them, not comprehending.

The first object exploded with a loud bang and the vampires felt a fine white spray across their faces. Then in quick succession the other objects exploded with the same effect.

The vampires sniffed the air and came to a terrible realisation – they were soaked from head to tail in garlic. They recoiled in disgust and panic as they flapped their wings to try to escape the ghastly smell. The more they flapped, the worse it got. The fine hairs on their bodies were caked with garlic. They started to flee out of the window.

The other vampires on the walls and in the garden couldn't make out what was going on, but seeing their routed leaders flying away in panic, they did the same. The whole swarm that had surrounded the house began fleeing and before long they had all disappeared into the distance.

The children only had a moment to savour their victory, before the bedroom door was flung open and Tich's mum in the most formidable anger entered.

'Right, that's it. I've had enough of all this. You're all going home.' She paused. 'And what is that terrible smell?'

'We threw Garlic Grenades,' explained the Boff.

For a moment Tich's mum was speechless. But not for long.

'You've been doing what?'

'Throwing Garlic Grenades.'

'Throwing Garlic Grenades. I've never heard

anything like it in my life. And I suppose Mr Van Heslop, or whatever his name is, gave you those as well. Right, well I'm going to have a word with this Heslop and give him a peace of my mind.'

'He probably died about a hundred years ago,' said the Boff

'Have you children been taking drugs or something? Your heads are full of such rubbish. All of you children – home! Now! Kevin get the dustpan and brush and clear this room up. You are not going out ever again. Really, you are such a disappointment to me. If only you'd been a girl. We could have gone shopping together and swapped make-up hints. But, no, I have to have a son who insists on having mad adventures all the time. It's all getting too much.'

The children looked at the floor. 'And now I've missed an entire episode of "Kerb that Dog".'

'Sorry,' said the children.

'Never mind sorry. Off home with the lot of you.'

Chapter Twenty-Nine

Ping Pong, Anyone Home?

It was five thirty in the morning and the sky was beginning to lighten as the dawn approached. At the far corner of the graveyard, seven children armed to the teeth with stakes, a saw, garlic bread, crucifixes and a gun that fired ping pong balls, which Ginger had insisted on bringing even though just how effective ping pong balls were against vampires was a factor largely unknown.

They kept themselves out of sight in the corner and were silent but alert.

The almost full moon was still visible on the horizon.

Suddenly Maggs hissed, 'There. Up there. Look.' They looked up at the dirty pink sky and saw what looked at first like a huge eagle, gliding just above the horizon.

'It's him,' said Tich. 'Get ready.'

The object followed a lazy arc gradually approaching the trees in the graveyard until eventually it swooped down to an elegant landing on the gravel path. It flapped its huge black wings and then retracted them until they disappeared behind its back. The hairy features changed and morphed into a smartly-dressed figure in a black cloak. The face the children recognised at once

'It's Draclea,' whispered Ginger.

'It can't be. It must be someone different. When we saw him it was two hundred years ago,' said the Boff.

'They live forever, remember,' said Tich.

'Nobody can live forever,' countered the Boff.

'But we buried him under the tower. We dumped about a million tons of rock on his head,' said Pigboy.

'We didn't stake him though, did we?' said Tich. 'That's the only way to stop them.'

'What's he doing here?' asked Maggs.

'In the book,' said the Boff.

'What book?'

'In *Dracula*. He comes over to England to get away from all the people that were after him. It's just a book though. It's not true.'

'What is that, if it isn't Dracula?' asked Tich. 'Look.'

Dracula was walking through the early morning mist approaching his hiding place in the mausoleum.

'When do we get him?'

'Not yet. We wait till he's back in his grave.'

Dracula entered the mausoleum and closed the door behind him. Pigboy stood up and moved forward, but Tich grabbed his arm. 'Not yet. Give him a minute.'

'Why, what's he doing – putting his pyjamas on?' asked Pigboy sarcastically.

'We want him lying down with his eyes shut,' said Tich. 'You know how strong he is. He could kill all of us easy.'

Pigboy waited impatiently until Tich gave the signal and they walked towards the mausoleum, keeping on the grass because the gravel would be too noisy. Finally they all gathered round the stone door. Maggs pushed her fingers into the gap and pulled the door open slowly and she peered inside. Dracula was nowhere to be seen. He had obviously laid down in his grave and pulled the stone slab back over him.

The children gathered around the tomb. Tich had the stake in his hand and Pigboy held the mallet.

'Ready,' said Tich. The children nodded their heads. 'Now.'

Maggs and Thicko pushed hard against the stone slab which, at first, refused to move but then it gave way and swung open with a loud grating sound. It was enough to wake the dead.

Dracula's cold, grey-white face shone out from the dark. His eyes were closed. His mouth was stained red, looking almost as if he had just been eating strawberries, but they all knew that it wasn't strawberries he'd been devouring.

'OK?' said Tich. He took the stake and placed it directly over Dracula's heart. Pigboy, who was by far the strongest of the children, stepped up with the mallet. 'Just watch my fingers,' said Tich.

Pigboy touched the stake with his mallet, and then swung it back over his head. Then, with a grunt, he brought it smashing down but the mallet didn't hit the centre of the stake. It caught it a glancing blow on the edge and then slipped off, narrowly missing Tich's fingers.

The blow was not enough to pierce the Vampire's flesh but it was enough to wake it up. The eyelids opened to reveal bloodshot eyes and the Vampire leapt out of the coffin and onto its feet.

Red-stained saliva was pouring from its mouth. Although they recognised it was Dracula, it was more like an animal now – a cross between a cobra about to strike and a rabid dog. It hissed and squealed and bared its teeth. The children were frozen in fear.

The Vampire grabbed Maggs and Thicko and threw them against the wall. Then it hit out at Pigboy knocking him to the ground. It tore the stake out of Tich's hand and struck a blow across his head, knocking him hard across the room. Barf and the Boff were scrabbling at the door trying to escape but the Vampire grabbed their legs and yanked them back. It swung them around and let go smashing them against Tich who was already lying on the floor, groaning.

The Vampire was breathing heavily as it inspected the children scattered across the floor. It did not see Ginger hidden behind the tomb. It leant forward and grabbed Tich with one hand and lifted him up. Tich gagged at the terrible fetid breath on his face. The Vampire bared its fangs and prepared to bite into Tich's throat.

'Put him down,' came a voice and the Vampire looked up. Ginger stood there with his ping-pong gun. The Vampire had never seen such a device. It released Tich from its grip, dropping him on to the ground barely conscious. The Vampire circled around eyeing Ginger suspiciously. Seeing the way Ginger's hands were shaking told the Vampire it was in no danger from the ping-pong gun. As it moved forward, Ginger began blasting away.

The Vampire, seeing the way the ping pong balls were bouncing harmlessly off its chest, began laughing – a deep guttural sound that chilled the soul. Soon it was roaring with laughter, tilting its head back and forward, until the tears were running down its cheeks. It was having trouble getting its breath, but Ginger kept on firing, determined to protect his friends.

Soon there was only one ping-pong ball left. Ginger aimed it at Dracula's head and, just as the Vampire was taking a deep breath and trying to regain its composure, he fired. The ping-pong ball was sucked into the Vampire's mouth where it disappeared, deep into its windpipe.

The Vampire coughed and spluttered and staggered from side to side, but the ping-pong ball was firmly stuck and would not be dislodged. The Vampire was coughing and wheezing , grasping at its throat, trying to catch its breath. It fell to its knees making weird gasping noises and then collapsed unconscious to the floor.

It lay on the ground twitching violently until finally it stopped moving altogether. When it seemed safe, the children gathered around the now unmoving figure. Pigboy poked it with his foot but there was no sign of life.

'Right,' said Pigboy. 'Let's get Dracula back in the grave and finish the job off properly this time.'

It took all of them to lift the body of the Vampire back into the stone grave but, with one large push, it tumbled in.

Once again Tich placed the stake against the Vampire's heart and Pigboy prepared to swing the mallet.

Chapter Thirty

Head and Safety

'Just what do you think you're doing?' came a voice from the door. The children froze. Daggers and the Vicar came striding into the mausoleum.

'Well? What are you all up to?' asked the Vicar.

'Er, nothing,' said Barf.

'We're just … killing … this vampire,' said Ginger.

'It was you lot with the spray paint before, wasn't it,' said Daggers. 'I seen you,' he said, addressing Pigboy. 'Always up to no good. What's it now – defiling the graves. Is there nothing you won't stoop to? All of you outside now.'

The children trooped out one by one and stood on the gravel path.

'Look,' said Tich, stepping forward. 'We're not vandals. There's a vampire in there. We think it might be Dracula. And we have to kill it today. There's a full moon tonight and if it's not dead by then, all the people it's bitten will become vampires, forever. We've only got this one chance to save them all and we've got to do it today.'

'And who told you this?'

'It doesn't matter,' said Tich.

'Of course it matters,' said Daggers.

'It was someone called Van Helsing,' explained Tich.

The Vicar and Daggers looked at each other and without saying a word they took the stake and the mallet and the saw and disappeared back into the mausoleum.

After a few moments the children heard a thump followed by several more. Then there was a sawing sound that went on for some ages which was finished by a muffled thump. The Vicar and Daggers then emerged from the mausoleum, their hands and clothes covered in blood. They pushed the stone door to and put communion wafers into the gaps in the door.

'We're going to have to seal this door once and for all you know,' said Daggers to the Vicar. 'We should have done it years ago.'

The Vicar addressed the children: 'What do you know about people breaking into this tomb and leaving spray paint everywhere?'

The children looked at the ground. 'If you children kept out of my graveyard,' he continued, 'none of this would have happened.' He paused. 'We'll keep all this that's gone on here to ourselves. Do you understand? I don't want my graveyard overrun with tourists.'

The children nodded their heads. 'Then go home and keep away from my churchyard in future.'

The children filed away and out through the churchyard gate.

'You do know,' said Pigboy to Tich, 'that just 'cause we killed Dracula, that doesn't mean we're friends. When we get back to school, things'll just be the same as they always were. We'll still be taking your money and your sweets. I can't let you off. I mean, I'd like to, but it just wouldn't be fair to the others.'

'Yeah I know,' said Tich.

'Just one thing,' said the Boff to Pigboy. 'That Chinese Burn thing you do. Could you stop doing that to me. It really hurts.'

'OK,' said Pigboy. 'Just don't tell anyone I've let you off.'

And with that Pigboy, Barf and Thicko headed off in one direction and the Boff, Maggs, Ginger and Tich in another.

The early morning traffic was beginning to flow and another day was beginning. Hundreds of people woke up to find they didn't need sunglasses anymore.

And none of them knew how close they'd been to spending the rest of eternity as vampires or how they'd all been saved by seven funny looking kids.

Chapter Thirty-One

Tich the Hero

Tich had just left his house on his way to school when he noticed Abigail Mountford coming up the path outside her house. He glanced at her briefly but as usual did not catch her eye for fear of turning cherry red and losing his chance with her forever.

As he walked along the road he sensed she was catching up with him, whereas usually she took no notice of him at all. Usually it was just as if Tich just wasn't there.

Out of the corner of his eye he caught a glimpse of her.

'Tich,' she said.

Tich turned round pretending he'd only just noticed her. 'Oh hello,' he said, all the time thinking *Don't go red. Don't go red*.

'Do you mind if I walk with you?'

Church bells began to ring in Tich's mind and church choirs began to sing.

'Yeah alright,' said Tich, desperately hanging on to his cool.

'I wanted to thank you.'

'What for?'

'For saving us, you know. If it wasn't for you, we'd all be vampires. We'd be like zombies. We'd spend all eternity as the Undead, living on human blood.'

'I didn't think anyone knew.'

'Most people don't, but I do.'

'It was nothing really. You know, we just had to kill this Dracula bloke and cut off his head and that.'

'No, no, you were fantastic. You're my hero.'

'Well, you know, it's just what you do, isn't it, you know, stuff.' Tich was starting to talk gibberish and needed to get a grip.

'Tich, stop.' Abigail put her hands on his shoulders. 'The thing is Tich, I love you, I want to marry you and live with you forever. Say yes Tich, please say yes.'

She leant down. Her face was moving towards his, turning just at an angle so that their noses didn't collide. Any second now their lips would meet and they would be together forever.

Then she said, 'Tich get out of bed. You'll be late for school.'

That's weird, thought Tich. That's a really weird thing to say. Why would she say that?

'Hurry up. Your breakfast is getting cold.'

None of this made sense. They were just going to kiss and suddenly Abigail started saying weird things in somebody else's voice.

Tich opened his eyes and looked at the wallpaper in his bedroom. It was some hideous blue pattern stuff his mum had insisted on. She'd said he was too old for Scooby Doo paper.

He'd been asleep and dreaming. The whole thing with Abigail was all in his mind. She didn't love him. She'd never noticed Tich and never would.

Tich sat up in bed and shouted out the most terrible, terrible swear word at the top of his voice.

'Is everything alright, Tich?' called out his mum.

'Yeah,' said Tich. 'Feppin brilliant.'